Trick or Treason by

Kathi Daley

D1739239

This book is a work of fiction. Names, characters, places, and incidents either are products of the author's imagination or are used fictitiously. Any resemblance to actual events or locales or persons, living or dead, is entirely coincidental.

Acknowledgments

I want to thank the very talented Jessica Fischer for the cover art.

I so appreciate Bruce Curran, who is always ready and willing to answer my cyber questions, Jayme Maness, who takes charge of book clubs and other reader events, and Peggy Hyndman, for helping sleuth out those pesky typos.

And, of course, thanks to the readers and bloggers in my life, who make doing what I do possible.

Thank you to Randy Ladenheim-Gil for the editing.

I also want to thank Sharon Guagliardo, Nancy Farris, Pam Curran, and Patty Liu for submitting recipes.

And finally I want to thank my sister Christy, for always lending an ear, and my husband Ken, for allowing me time to write by taking care of everything else.

Books by Kathi Daley

Zoe Donovan Cozy Mystery:

Halloween Hijinks
The Trouble With Turkeys
Christmas Crazy
Cupid's Curse
Big Bunny Bump-off
Beach Blanket Barbie
Maui Madness
Derby Divas
Haunted Hamlet
Turkeys, Tuxes, and Tabbies
Christmas Cozy
Alaskan Alliance
Matrimony Meltdown
Soul Surrender
Heavenly Honeymoon
Hopscotch Homicide
Ghostly Graveyard
Santa Sleuth
Shamrock Shenanigans
Kitten Kaboodle
Costume Catastrophe
Candy Cane Caper
Holiday Hangover
Easter Escapade
Camp Carter
Trick or Treason
Reindeer Roundup – *December 2017*

Zimmerman Academy The New Normal

Tj Jensen Paradise Lake Mysteries by Henery Press

Pumpkins in Paradise
Snowmen in Paradise
Bikinis in Paradise
Christmas in Paradise
Puppies in Paradise
Halloween in Paradise
Treasure in Paradise
Fireworks in Paradise – *October 2017*

Whales and Tails Cozy Mystery:

Romeow and Juliet
The Mad Catter
Grimm's Furry Tail
Much Ado About Felines
Legend of Tabby Hollow
Cat of Christmas Past
A Tale of Two Tabbies
The Great Catsby
Count Catula
The Cat of Christmas Present
A Winter's Tail
The Taming of the Tabby
Frankencat
The Cat of Christmas Future – *November 2017*

Seacliff High Mystery:

The Secret
The Curse
The Relic
The Conspiracy
The Grudge
The Shadow
The Haunting

Sand and Sea Hawaiian Mystery:

Murder at Dolphin Bay
Murder at Sunrise Beach
Murder at the Witching Hour
Murder at Christmas
Murder at Turtle Cove
Murder at Water's Edge
Murder at Midnight – *October 2017*

Writers' Retreat Southern Seashore Mystery:

First Case
Second Look
Third Strike
Fourth Victim – *October 2017*

Rescue Alaska Paranormal Mystery:

Finding Justice – *November 2017*

A Tess and Tilly Cozy Mystery
The Christmas Letter – *December 2017*

Road to Christmas Romance:
Road to Christmas Past

Chapter 1

Monday, October 23

"I think I first realized I was in trouble when the marshmallow ghost decided to lead an attack against the Milky Way king. I remember grabbing my candy corn shield as I prepared for what was to come, but when the Raisinets began to rain down on the entire candy kingdom, I knew a shield made of candy corn wasn't going to be nearly enough."

"Sounds terrifying," my best friend, Ellie Denton, replied as she tossed a bag of Snickers into her basket. We were shopping at the Halloween store in preparation for the upcoming holiday.

"It really was," I confirmed, my heart still racing at the memory of the dream I'd had the previous night.

Ellie handed her six-month-old son, Eli, one of the small stuffed pumpkins she'd picked up from a nearby bin. "So what did you do once you realized the entire world was about to be covered in Raisinets?"

"The only thing I could. I dove into the chocolate sea and swam for my life. What do you think it means?"

Ellie turned toward me with a smile. "I think it means Catherine wants you to lay off the Chinese takeout so close to bedtime."

I put my hand on the small bump under my loose-fitting T-shirt. "You think?"

Ellie laughed and grabbed my hand in hers. "I do. I have to hand it to you, Zoe Donovan-Zimmerman; you've been experiencing the most entertaining pregnancy symptoms of anyone I've ever met."

"Lucky me." I groaned as I pressed my hands into the small of my back.

"Is your back still hurting?" Ellie asked with genuine sympathy in her voice.

"It has been. I guess I knew back pain would be part of the pregnancy package, but I'm only a couple of weeks into my third trimester. If my back hurts this badly so early in the game I can't imagine what it's going to feel like when I reach my ninth month."

"Have you talked to your doctor?"

I nodded. "He told me to slow down a bit. Like I can even consider doing such a thing. Haunted Hamlet is next weekend and I don't have nearly enough volunteers lined up for the kiddie events, the Halloween dance at Zimmerman Academy is on Friday and I still need to get Alex a dress, and Scooter's soccer team entered a tournament that starts on Wednesday." I referred to Scooter Sherwood and Alex Bremmerton, the two thirteen-year-olds who lived with my husband Zak and me.

"You do have a lot on your plate," Ellie admitted.

"If that was all I had to worry about I might be fine, but to top it all off, the guy from the county is coming this week to do his final inspection on the remodel at the Zoo," I said, referring to the wild and domestic animal rescue and rehabilitation shelter I owned. "I know Jeremy is on top of things, but still, I worry. We have two additional bear cubs coming in two weeks to winter with us and we're already at capacity. I don't know what we'll do if we can't open the new wing."

"It'll be fine," Ellie assured me. "Jeremy is a fantastic manager and he knows what he's doing."

I did agree that Jeremy Fisher had matured quite a lot from the nineteen-year-old I originally hired five years ago when I still worked for the county.

"Do you think these leaves will look good around the front window of the boathouse?" Ellie asked.

I looked at the garland of red, yellow, and orange leaves. "I think they'll look really nice. You might want to put some around the door as well."

"Yeah, that's a good idea." Ellie tossed the leaves in her basket and then continued on to the costumes. Now that the remodel on the boathouse was complete, this was going to be her first Halloween in her new home and Ellie was going all out, it seemed.

"Zak is in the midst of his usual decorating crazies. The exterior of the house looks like a haunted wonderland, but there's still a lot to do on the inside. Personally, I hope he scales back a bit. I'm exhausted just watching him do his magic and we've barely entered the holiday season."

"Zak does tend to go all out with the decorating," Ellie said. "Of course, he goes all out in everything he does. Now, I want to concentrate the rest of my energy on a costume. I think I might dress up as Elvira this year. Last year I needed to cover up my figure, but this year I think I'll show it off. Carrying Eli around has done wonderful things to my arms."

"That'll look nice," I said enviously. I had no idea what I was going to dress up as this year. I was pretty much to the point in my pregnancy where I simply looked fat, which wasn't a good look on my small frame, so I supposed I'd go as a ghost or some other figure-forgiving costume.

I watched as Ellie picked up a fuzzy costume and held it up in front of her adorable offspring. "You aren't going to dress Eli as Elmo, are you?"

Ellie looked down at the costume. "I was thinking about it. Is there a problem with Elmo?"

"He's just so red."

"And that's bad because...?"

I let out a long sigh. "Red is just a darker shade of pink."

"Are you still duking it out with Mother Zimmerman about the color of the nursery?"

"The woman is definitely a paint swatch away from sending me over the edge," I grumbled.

Ellie returned the Elmo costume to the rack and picked up a Cookie Monster one. "How do you feel about blue?"

"Blue is fine. I've always liked blue and I used to like red. I'm actually fairly outraged that Mother Zimmerman ruined red for me."

"And how did that happen exactly?" Ellie placed a black wig on her head and studied herself in the mirror.

"She designed a nursery decorated entirely in pink and white and then *surprised* me with an interior designer who just showed up on our doorstep with a van full of paint, wallpaper, bedding, and furniture. You know how I feel about pink?"

"I do. Pink is the devil. I thought Zak talked to his mom and explained the whole pink-is-evil thing."

"He did. I thought it was taken care of until the designer showed up with all the same items, only in a deep rose shade. Mother Zimmerman insists it's red, but I know dark pink when I see it. There's no way my daughter is going to spend the first months of her life in a prissy pink room."

Ellie placed her hand over her mouth. She pretended to cough, but I could see she was suppressing a chuckle.

"It's not funny," I insisted.

"Actually, it kinda is."

"What am I going to do? The woman is driving me crazy and she hasn't even shown up yet for her live reign of terror."

"When is she coming?"

I let out a long breath. "I don't know exactly. She keeps moving it up. First it was going to be after Christmas, and then she decided that as long as she was making the trip she may as well be in Ashton Falls for the holiday. The last I heard she was planning on arriving in mid-December, but I won't be surprised if she's in town by Thanksgiving. I don't know how I'm going to deal with her once she does arrive. I know she's Zak's mother, and I know I need to find a way to make peace with her, but she's just so dang nosy and bossy. No matter how hard I try to keep my cool she turns me into a crazy woman. Combine that with the pregnancy hormones and I actually think I might be capable of committing murder."

"You might not want to say that quite so loudly, but I do agree that she seems to have a way of pushing your buttons."

"Catherine is my daughter. I want to design the nursery. With Zak's input, of course. This should be a fun project we can work on together, but instead the whole thing is giving me indigestion."

Ellie replaced the wig and continued to the aisle with orange lights and rubber spiders. "Have you talked to Zak about your desire to decorate the nursery on your own?"

"I have."

"And…?"

"And he said he'll handle his mom."

"Is there any reason you don't believe him?"

I picked up a large rubber bat and tossed it into my own basket. "No." I sighed. "He told me to choose any color I want and he would make sure nothing other than that color touched the nursery walls."

"It sounds like your wonderful, thoughtful husband has it handled, so I really don't see the problem."

I started to cry.

"You have a counterpoint?"

"I don't know what color to choose," I sobbed. At that moment it really hit me hard that Zoe Donovan-Zimmerman had officially given in to the baby bump blues.

******

"Better?" Ellie asked me a short while later after she'd ushered me out of the Halloween store and led me down the street to Rosie's, where she ordered us each a cup of soup and a loaf of warm bread to share.

I glanced at Eli, who was sleeping in his stroller. "I'm better, but I'm pretty sure your baby is a felon."

Ellie frowned until I pointed to the fuzzy pumpkin Eli still clung to but Ellie hadn't waited to pay for. "Oops. I guess I'll need to go back when we're done here."

I took a sip of my soup, sat back in the booth, and felt myself relax. It was nice to be out with my best friend on a weekday evening with nothing more to do than look at the fantastic decorations the town had put out. "I have the strangest feeling of déjà vu, only last year it was you having the meltdown in the Halloween store and me ushering you out the door and down the street to Rosie's."

"I guess we have come full circle," Ellie said. "Let's just hope we don't receive a cryptic message leading to a murder mystery this year."

"Yeah. I could do with a murder-free holiday for once. I don't know why I'm letting everything get to me. I love Halloween. I should just sit back and enjoy the season."

"I agree, you should. Catherine needs you to relax a bit."

"That's exactly what my doctor said, and Zak has been worried that I'm so on edge all the time. I think if I can make a decision on the nursery once and for all I'll feel a bit more settled."

"Okay, so let's talk about it." Ellie buttered a piece of the bread and popped a corner of it into her mouth. "I know pink is evil and you've lost your fondness for red, but there are a lot of other very nice colors."

"Yeah, but which one?"

"Maybe you should start with a theme."

I considered that. "That might be a good idea. Maybe something with animals. I think a room filled with soft, fluffy stuffed animals would be fun. Maybe Noah's Ark or the zoo. Or maybe an enchanted forest with cute baby animals."

"I love that idea." Ellie smiled. "You can have a mural painted on one wall. There could even be fairies hidden among the trees. That would give it a girly feel without suffering a pink explosion, and maybe the other walls could be a neutral color that would complement the forest scene, like pale blue or pale green. And Mother Zimmerman already bought white furniture, which would look very nice, and it wouldn't clash with the animal theme."

I smiled. "While I find myself resisting using Mother Zimmerman's crib, it really is very nice, and it has a matching dresser, changing table, bookshelf, and rocking chair. I love your suggestion for the mural, and using her furniture would help to smooth things over with her."

"It would be fun to shop for cute bedding for the crib. I can even make something if you can't find exactly what you want."

I grinned. "Okay. It looks like we have a plan. Thank you. Suddenly, I feel much better. In fact, I think I'm going to splurge on dessert. Order me a piece of pumpkin pie. I need to run to the ladies' room."

"Whipped cream?"

"Of course," I answered as I slipped out of the booth.

Spending the evening with Ellie was exactly what I'd needed. She knew me well enough that she always said exactly what would make me feel better. Not only did I finally have a vision for the nursery that I loved, but I felt more relaxed than I had in weeks. When Zak and I had decided to try for a baby I'd promised myself that I wouldn't be one of those weepy, emotional women who stressed out over every little thing, but so far that was exactly what I'd been. But that ended today, I decided, as I walked down the hallway to find a line at the bathroom door.

"I hope you aren't in a hurry," the woman I fell into line behind commented. "There are two teenage girls in there and despite our frequent knocks on the door they seem to be taking their own sweet time."

"Are you sure they're okay?" I asked.

"They're fine. Every now and then I can hear giggling."

There were two women in front of the woman in front of me. I didn't want to wait around for the girls to finish and the three women in line to have their turn. After a moment of indecision, I decided to sneak out the back through the door leading from the kitchen to the alley, and then head next door to Bears and Beavers, where I knew store owner Gilda Reynolds would let me use her ladies' room.

I stepped out of the kitchen door and into the alley, where I almost tripped over something laying just beyond the threshold. I bent down to take a closer look at the item, which appeared to be a blanket with something wrapped inside, when I noticed a human foot peeking out the other end. I slowly lifted the edge of the blanket closest to where I knelt, before taking my phone out of my pocket and calling Sheriff Salinger. It looked like a murder-free holiday wasn't going to be in my future after all.

Chapter 2

"Who is it?" Ellie asked after I texted her to tell her why I hadn't returned to the booth and she joined me in the alley.

"Willa Walton."

Ellie put her hand to her mouth. "Oh God. What happened?"

"It looks like blunt force trauma to the head. I only took a peek to make sure the person wrapped in the blanket was actually dead and not in need of help, so I don't know a lot. I guess we'll know more when Salinger gets here."

"Who would do such a thing?" Ellie asked as tears streamed down her face.

I wiped away my own tears with the back of my hand. "I don't know." I glanced at the stroller, where Eli was still sleeping. "Listen, I'm going to be a while. Salinger should be here any minute and Zak is on his way. Why don't you go ahead and take Eli home? I'll stop by the boathouse to fill you and Levi in when I'm done here."

"Are you sure?"

I nodded. "I'm sure. A murder scene is no place for a baby."

Ellie hugged me and then headed back into the restaurant just as Salinger pulled up. I'd known Willa Walton for years. She was not only the chairperson for the events committee Levi, Eli, Zak, and I were on but she'd been the town clerk for as long as I could remember. Willa was an organized if somewhat stringent person who came off as being formal and rigid until you got to know her and realized that beneath the staunch exterior was a woman with a warm and loving heart.

"So what do we know?" Salinger asked as he pulled on a pair of gloves and knelt next to the victim.

"Not a lot. Ellie and I were having dinner at Rosie's. I needed to use the ladies' room, but there was a line at the door in there, so I decided to sneak out the back to use the facilities at Bears and Beavers. I almost tripped over the blanket on my way out the door, so I bent over to move it aside when I saw a human foot sticking out at the bottom. I lifted the top of the blanket to make sure the person inside wasn't in need of medical attention and then called you."

Salinger removed a larger section of the blanket. He touched a hand to Willa's face and gently turned her head to the side. "It looks like she's only been dead a short time. Less than an hour." Salinger looked around the alley. "There isn't a lot of blood, so it appears she was killed elsewhere, wrapped in the blanket, and dumped here."

"Why would anyone do that? It seems to me that if you're going to go to all the trouble to move a body you'd dump it where it wouldn't be easily found, not on the threshold of a busy restaurant."

Salinger looked back down at the body. He took Willa's arm in his hand and turned it over. "There's blood on her hands and it looks like skin under her fingernails. I'm going to go out on a limb and say she fought with her attacker. We should be able to pull DNA. She's still wearing her work clothes, so I'm going to assume she was either still at work or just leaving when she was attacked. As soon as reinforcements show up, I'll head over to the town offices."

I took a deep breath and let it out slowly. This couldn't be happening. Salinger's arrival must have alerted the kitchen staff that something was going on because a crowd was beginning to gather at Rosie's back door. I was debating whether I should volunteer to handle crowd control when Zak pulled up.

"Are you okay?" Zak asked after parking in the alley and making his way to where I was standing with Salinger.

"I'm fine. I still do need to use the ladies' room, so maybe you can help Salinger. I'll pop into Bears and Beavers. It won't be as crowded as the restaurant."

"I'm going to need to secure this area," Salinger said. "Tell Gilda to prevent anyone from coming out to the alley through her back door." He looked at Zak. "If you could do the same for the restaurant that would be helpful."

"Certainly," Zak replied. "Whatever you need."

I slipped into Bears and Beavers and used the ladies' room before I did anything else. Ever since I'd been pregnant it seemed I had to pee every half hour. Once I'd taken care of my bodily needs I headed to the front of the store, where Gilda was chatting with a customer.

"Zoe, how are you, dear?"

"I'm fine. Can I talk to you for a minute?" I glanced at the woman Gilda was speaking to in the hope that she would understand our conversation needed to be private.

"Of course, dear. What is it?"

"I should be on my way," the customer said before I could say anything. "I'll catch up with you next week."

"That would be fine, and I'll call you if the canisters come in."

Once the woman left I suggested Gilda put out her "Closed" sign and lock her front door.

"What is it, dear?" Gilda asked, obvious concern in her voice by this point.

"It's Willa."

"What's wrong with Willa?"

"I'm afraid she's dead."

******

The next thirty minutes seemed to fly by as Zak secured the alley and I tried to calm the hysterical owner of Bears and Beavers. Once reinforcements showed up to help Salinger monitor the area, Zak and I were released to go home. The sheriff promised to call me when he had something to report, so I let Zak lead me to his truck.

He took my hand in his and wound his fingers through mine. "Are you sure you're okay?" he asked before turning the key in the ignition.

"I feel a bit dazed," I admitted. "I know Willa can be prickly, but I can't imagine why anyone would want her dead."

"Salinger will figure it out."

I lay my head back against the seat and closed my eyes. God, I was tired. "Yeah. I guess." A tear slid out from beneath my lid and traveled down my cheek. "I told Ellie we'd come by. She was pretty upset, but she knew it was best to take Eli home."

"Okay," Zak said, turning the key in the ignition. He backed up and then made his way slowly down the alley past the emergency vehicles that had blocked both ends. "Do you want to text Ellie to let her know we're on our way?"

"Yeah, that's a good idea." I took out my phone. "I guess I should also text Scooter and Alex to let them know we'll be late getting home."

"They were both working on homework when I left the house and I told them we might be late, but it still might be a good idea to text them. I'm sure they'll be worried."

"Did Scooter finish his history project? It's due tomorrow."

"Alex and I helped him after dinner. By the time you called all he had left to do was his reading and Alex was working on her computer."

"And the dogs?"

"I took them all out shortly before you called, so they should be fine until we get home."

It sounded like everything was handled, at least for the moment, so I let myself relax as we drove toward the newly remodeled boathouse where Levi, Ellie, and baby Eli lived. Orange twinkle lights shone brightly from the trees along the drive and there were colorful scarecrows dotting the scenery at random intervals. Zak parked near the front door and then helped me out.

"The place looks nice," Zak commented, I was sure to lighten the mood.

"Yeah, Ellie's really into the whole decorating thing this year. I think you might have a rival for the title of decorating king—or, in Ellie's case, queen.

Zak smiled as he put his arm around my shoulders. "Ellie's done a good job, but she's an amateur and therefore no rival for the Halloween king."

The light mood Zak was trying to manifest lasted only until we reached the front door and Ellie pulled me into her arms. Despite the tears we'd already shed, I found myself sobbing for the friend and neighbor we'd lost. After a few minutes she took a step back and ushered me inside. She must have realized I'd never finished my dinner because she had soup and sandwiches waiting. The three nonpregnant adults shared a bottle of wine while I made do with milk served in a wineglass.

"What did Salinger think happened?" Levi asked after we'd all settled around the dining table. I didn't see Eli, so I assumed he'd already been put to bed. Levi and Ellie's dogs, Shep and Karloff, were napping together near the new fireplace that had been part of the remodel.

"He wasn't sure yet," I answered. "He's fairly certain Willa was killed elsewhere, wrapped in the blanket, and then left in the alley."

"That's nuts," Levi voiced the same sentiment I'd already expressed. "Why would you dump a body near Rosie's back door if that wasn't where the murder had taken place?"

"I don't know yet, but I'd consider it significant, not random. Salinger also said Willa had blood on her hands and skin under her fingernails, so she must have fought back. I'm sure once he locates the actual murder scene and has the opportunity to test the skin for DNA, he'll be able to narrow things down quite a bit."

Ellie hadn't said much since we'd sat down, but I could tell there was something on her mind.

"Are you okay?" I asked her. She'd known Willa as long as I had, and in some ways was closer to her. Ellie was close to a lot of people because she made it a point to be friendly to everyone she came into contact with on a regular basis.

"I keep thinking back to last week's events committee meeting. I could tell something was going on with Willa then," Ellie eventually answered.

"It's true that last Tuesday was the first time I ever remember Willa being late and she did seem distracted," I said. "Do you think her behavior is related to what happened this evening?"

Ellie shrugged. "Maybe. Have you seen or spoken to her at all since last Tuesday?"

I paused to consider. "I haven't seen her, but she sent me an email last Friday. She wanted a list of the volunteers I'd lined up for Haunted Hamlet. I sent them to her, along with a note informing her that I felt like we were going to come up short. She responded by saying she'd try to recruit some additional people to help. She also informed me that she might miss this week's committee meeting, which would have been tomorrow, and wondered if I could get an update from all the committee chairs. I said I would, and that was the last time I communicated with her."

"Did she give any indication of why she thought she might miss the meeting?" Levi asked.

"No. It didn't even seem like she was definitely going to miss it. It was more like there was a chance she might; I didn't get the impression it was something she definitely planned on."

"Today is Monday and the county offices are open, and it wasn't yet six o'clock when Zoe first found Willa's body, so Willa must have either been at work or just leaving work when she was attacked," Levi commented.

"Salinger made the same comment and said he planned to check the town offices first thing."

"Should we call people about tomorrow's meeting?" Ellie asked. "Should we still hold it or should we cancel?"

"We do still have the Hamlet this weekend," I pointed out. "Tomorrow's meeting is the last one before the event, so I think we need to make sure everyone is ready. I know it seems sort of cold to go ahead with the meeting so soon after Willa's death, but we all know how much the Hamlet meant to her and how much it means to the financial health of the town. I think if she could communicate with us, Willa would tell us to proceed as planned."

"I agree," Ellie chimed in.

"I'd say we should email people to let them know what happened so they aren't blindsided tomorrow," Zak suggested. "Although I'm not sure Salinger wants Willa's death to be public knowledge at this point."

"Gilda knows," I said. "The staff and customers at Rosie's know. Chances are anyone in town this evening would have seen the emergency vehicles and asked what happened, and I'd assume those in the know would have filled everyone else in. I doubt Willa's death is a secret."

"I think Zak is right about emailing everyone," Levi joined in.

"There are only ten committee members now including Willa, which leaves nine," I said. "The four of us know and Gilda knows, which just leaves my dad, Hazel, Tawny, and Paul. I'll just call them. I think it will be better to let them know with a phone call than an email."

"We'll help you," Ellie offered. "Zoe, you can call Hazel because she'll most likely take it the hardest, Zak can call your dad, I'll call Tawny, and Levi will call Paul."

"I think Grandpa is at Hazel's tonight, so I'll talk to him as well," I volunteered. I hated to ruin date night for my grandpa and the librarian he'd found love with so late in life, but I knew they'd want to know and I figured it was best they heard it from me. Willa knew a lot of people, but if I had to designate a single person as Willa's best friend I was sure it would be Hazel. Ellie was right; she was going to take it hard.

Chapter 3

Tuesday, October 24

The group that met the next morning was somber indeed. Levi got a substitute for his classes so he could show up early with Zak, Ellie, and me. My mom had agreed to babysit Eli and my dad offered to pick up both Hazel and Grandpa. Grandpa wasn't officially a member of the group, but I knew he wanted to be there to support Hazel. Tawny Upton, the owner of Over the Rainbow Preschool, showed up shortly after we arrived, followed by a puffy-eyed Gilda, who must have been working out her grief with baking because she brought enough cookies to feed the entire town.

"Has anyone spoken to Paul?" I asked about Paul Iverson, the only committee member who had not yet arrived.

"When I spoke to him last night he said he'd be here. He may have been held up with a client," Levi volunteered.

Paul was a psychologist and often did arrive late to the meetings.

"Okay, then, I think we should get started," I suggested. "We're going to need a new committee leader. Would anyone like to volunteer?"

No one jumped in, so I suggested we table the discussion until the next meeting. It seemed like discussing the Hamlet was the most important topic for today.

"Does anyone know exactly what happened?" Tawny asked before we could even get started.

"Sheriff Salinger said he'd call me with an update when he knew something, but so far I haven't heard a thing," I answered. "All I know is that Willa was hit on the head with a blunt object, wrapped in a blanket, and dumped in the alley."

"I'm really having a hard time with this," Hazel admitted. "When I spoke to her yesterday afternoon I had a sense that something was wrong, but I was busy and didn't take the time to dig deeper, and now she's dead. I can't help but wonder if she might still be alive if I'd dropped everything and walked next door to see what was up." The library where Hazel worked was next to the county offices where Willa had worked.

"You couldn't have known what would happen," Grandpa tried to comfort her.

"Maybe not, but that doesn't mean I shouldn't have taken a moment to check on a friend who seemed to be having a difficult day."

"Did Willa say anything that would indicate what was wrong, or did you notice anyone or anything yesterday that seemed odd or out of place?" I asked Hazel.

I could tell by the expression on Hazel's face that she was considering my question. "I know she'd been going round and round with Porky Walfer. Porky built a deck onto the back of his house, but one entire section of the structure is over the property line. As you know, if you live in the town limits and you want to add a deck onto your home, you're supposed to have the land surveyed and apply for a permit. Porky didn't do either. Willa insisted that he remove the part of the deck that was on forest service land, but he was adamant that his deck wasn't hurting anything and Willa should just leave it be."

"I take it she wasn't going to let it be?" I asked.

"No, she wasn't. In fact, I think she not only arranged to have Porky fined for failing to get a permit but she was planning to take legal action to have the deck torn down."

"Sounds like a motive for murder to me," Tawny suggested.

"Maybe," I agreed. "I'll mention it to Salinger. Does anyone know anything else he should be made aware of?"

"He might want to speak to Cory Danielson," my dad, Hank Donovan, said. "I know Cory and Willa had a rather loud exchange of words in the parking lot in front of Donovan's the other day."

"Do you know what they were arguing about?" I asked.

"I was with a customer, so I didn't go out to see what was going on, but even from inside the store with the doors closed I could hear yelling and name-calling. Willa ended the conversation by getting into her car and driving away. I asked Cory if everything was okay and he said that other than the fact that Willa had plumb lost her mind, everything was fine.

Another customer came in and I decided to leave it alone."

"I think Cory and Willa might have been dating," Tawny supplied. "I don't know that for certain, but I've seen his car out in front of her place several times over the past few weeks."

Willa and Cory were both single and close to the same age, so I supposed a romantic relationship wasn't out of the question, although in terms of personality they didn't seem like a good fit at all.

"Does anyone else have anything?" I asked.

"Henrietta Toffer," Ellie said. "I don't know why I didn't think of this before, but I ran into Henrietta a couple of months ago and she told me that she was going to have to shut down her hair salon because she was behind on the local sales tax and Willa was insisting she pay up or close her doors. Henrietta told me that she was so far behind there was no way she could meet Willa's deadline. I felt sorry for Henrietta because I can remember how easy it was to get behind when I owned the Beach Hut, but I also understood it wasn't fair to let one person slide when everyone else managed to make their payments on time."

"Do you think Henrietta would actually kill Willa?" I asked. "She doesn't seem the violent type."

"I agree, but she has three other girls working in the salon. If she was forced to close they'd have to find a new place to work. One of the three is a very large woman with a body full of tats who just looks mean. I don't really know her, but I heard she used to be in a gang and was arrested. She moved to Ashton Falls after she got out of prison. I don't know her name, but Salinger could ask Henrietta."

"Okay, I'll let him know. Anything else?"

The room fell silent as everyone considered the situation. It seemed the energy in the room had changed once everyone began to participate in finding a solution. I could identify with that. I knew from prior experience the feeling of helplessness that could overtake you when someone you cared about had died, but I also knew that being involved in the solution to the problem was a good way to work through your grief.

"Someone should go by to look at Willa's desk calendar," Hazel suggested. "She kept a record of every appointment she made, every call needing a return, and every visitor who came by. It should tell us who the last person to see Willa alive might have been. It will at least tell us who her last appointment of the day was."

"We've come up with a lot of really good leads. I think I'm going to call Salinger right now." I glanced at Zak. "Maybe you can have everyone report on their level of readiness for the Hamlet. You can catch me up later."

Zak agreed and took over the conversation while I went outside to call Salinger. I not only wanted to find out what he knew; I wanted to fill him in on the leads we'd generated that morning as well. Luckily, he answered his personal cell, so I didn't have to take a chance on going through the main switchboard. Salinger's new receptionist was sort of prickly and often refused to put my calls through, insisting that I leave a message.

"We did look at Willa's desk calendar," Salinger informed me. "The last entry was one at five o'clock, which simply said *TJ*. I don't suppose you know who TJ might be?"

I paused to think about it. Tom, Tina, Tiffany, Ted, Tonya? People I knew with a first name beginning with a T seemed endless, but offhand, I couldn't think of anyone with a last name beginning with a

J. "Nothing comes to mind, but I'll think about it. Did anything else on the calendar stand out as seeming relevant?"

"Not really. I've been following up on a few things, but nothing has panned out. As for Cory Danielson, Porky Walfer, and Henrietta Toffer, I'll have chats with them. I want you to take a backseat on this one given your condition."

"I'm pregnant, not disabled, but I get what you're saying. I'll let you do the cop thing. Zak and I are both up for research if you need help with that."

"The medical examiner determined that the skin and blood under Willa's fingernails came from a female. There was also makeup—a medium shade of foundation to be exact. I sent a sample out for DNA testing, although we don't have anything to match it with. Still, you might be on the lookout for a Caucasian woman with scratch marks on her face."

"I'll do that. Did you locate the actual murder scene?" I asked.

"Not yet. There were no signs of a struggle at Willa's office or home. We located her car in town. It was parked in the public lot off Second Street. We didn't find evidence that the murder occurred in or near the car, and so far, we don't know why Willa was parked there."

"Okay, well, that's something. I'll see what I can find out. Willa was well known in the community. Someone must have seen her. Anything else?"

"We're trying to see if we can find any physical evidence on the blanket Willa was wrapped in. So far, we've pulled up dog hair from multiple dogs. It would seem the killer either has a lot of dogs or the blanket was somewhere multiple dogs would have had access to it."

I found this both odd and disturbing. Most dog lovers were peaceful people who would never hurt a flea. Or at least that was what I'd always told myself. I supposed dog owners ran the full gamut of personalities, including the less-than-pleasant ones. "Do you know what kind of dogs are associated with the hairs?"

"Not at this point."

"Do you mind if I come by to take a look? I am, after all, the queen of dog hair. If we can isolate the breeds with access to the blanket it might help us narrow things down."

"Fine by me. I'll be in the office until noon unless I get a call."

"Okay. Zak and I are at the events committee meeting. We'll come by afterward."

When I returned to the meeting the group was discussing the food vendors that were participating this year. Zak seemed to have a good handle on things, so I took a seat and allowed him to continue. It seemed as if everyone was on top of things, which I certainly hoped was true. I barely had time to follow up on my own commitment to the event, let alone do anything to track the others.

As soon as the meeting drew to a close, Zak and I made plans to have Levi, Ellie, and Eli over for dinner, and then we headed to Salinger's office. He was sitting at the reception desk chatting on the phone when we entered. He waved at us to have a seat, which we did. After a few minutes he hung up and turned his attention to us.

"So, you've come to look at dog hair."

"We have," I confirmed. "Not that I can replace DNA tests that are done in a lab, but I know my dog hair pretty well and I know my dog owners too. For example, if I were to find hair from a Tibetan terrier, a golden Lab, and a Newfoundland, I'd say the blanket belonged to me. If it had hair from a golden Lab, a golden retriever, a mixed breed terrier, and a springer spaniel, I'd say it belonged to my parents."

"You've convinced me. Come on back to my office."

Zak and I followed Salinger down the hall. The blanket was enclosed in a plastic bag. Salinger slipped on rubber gloves and handed me a pair as well. He removed the blanket from the bag and laid it out on a nearby table. I felt my stomach roll when I saw all the blood. I hadn't realized how much blood there would be, though I supposed I should have.

I took a deep breath and fought down the nausea. "Wow," I said after I considered the evidence in front of me. "You were right. There is hair from a lot of different dogs. I can see at least ten different breeds represented without looking all that closely: golden retriever, golden and chocolate Lab, pug, Irish setter, mixed breed terrier, and poodle. I can't think of a single person who would own so many dogs of so many different breeds, but I can think of several professions where you might have a single blanket that multiple dogs would use."

"Such as?"

"A dog walker who had the blanket in the back of their car. A dog groomer who provided a blanket for the dogs who were waiting. An animal control officer, if we lived somewhere other than here, where

Jeremy and I take care of that. Jeremy and I wash our blankets a lot more often than this one has been. There are dog breeders in the valley who have large numbers of dogs, but most breeders stick to one or two breeds, so I doubt it's that. Maybe a dog trainer who picks dogs up and takes them on location. If I were you I'd go through the local business licenses to see who has a business that meet these criteria."

"Okay. That's a good idea. I think there's a chance that whoever killed Willa did so because of a professional beef they had with her. She was a nice-enough woman and we got along all right, but she was a stickler for the rules. I can't tell you how many times she called me to arrest someone for some minor infraction of a random town code that most of the time I'd never heard of and had to look up."

Salinger had a point. I think once we really got into this investigation we were going to find that it wasn't a lack of suspects that was the problem but the huge number of people who had a problem with Willa.

"I agree with you, which is why I think you should jot down a list of the complaints you've received in recent weeks. I'll continue to ask around as well.

We got a few really good leads simply by asking the group gathered for the committee meeting. You might also want to talk to her neighbors. Tawny said she'd observed Cory Danielson's car outside Willa's house several times over the past few weeks. Her closest neighbors may have witnessed other cars coming and going."

Salinger chuckled. "This isn't my first pony show."

I shrugged. "I know. I guess sitting on the sidelines isn't really sitting well with me."

"Despite that, you do plan to watch from the sidelines," Zak emphasized. "Right?"

"Right. Catherine and I will let the two of you handle all the fun stuff. I can help, though. I can talk to people I know in public forums. Scooter has soccer tomorrow and there'll be a lot of people at the game and I have book club on Thursday. I think you'll be surprised how much I can come up with from the safety of the sidelines."

Salinger looked at Zak. "Seems like you might want to put a leash on her."

"Trust me, I'm seriously considering doing just that."

Chapter 4

After Zak and I left Salinger's office we headed to the deli to have lunch. After the initial chocoholic phase of my first trimester, I'd been trying to avoid greasy and sugary foods, so I ordered a turkey on whole wheat with a vegetable salad on the side.

"So where should we start?" I asked Zak, who looked very handsome today in a royal-blue sweatshirt that matched his eyes.

"Didn't I just hear you tell Salinger you were going to leave the cop thing to us?" he asked as we settled into a booth in the back.

"I did and I will."

Zak just stared at me.

"I'm not going to do the cop thing. I did think we might look around a bit, though."

"Isn't *looking around a bit* a cop thing?"

"Maybe, but it's also a reporter thing, a building inspector thing, a nosy neighbor thing. Really, looking around is an extremely general activity."

Zak let out a long breath. "Okay, I can see I'm not going to win this debate. What were you thinking?"

"Maybe we should head over to Willa's house to look around. Salinger might have missed something. You know how his eyesight has been off lately. Or, if you don't want to do that, we could go to the hardware store to talk to Porky. He seems like a real suspect in my mind, although I don't think he has any dogs. Or, if you prefer, we could just go straight over to Second Street after we're done eating. If Willa's car was left in the public lot she must have been visiting one of the businesses there. We'd be putting Catherine in absolutely no danger if we simply took a stroll and asked a few questions. Besides, I still need to buy Scooter some new cleats before tomorrow and there's a sporting goods store a block from the public lot."

Zak sat back, crossed his arms, and looked directly at me. "Are you sure there isn't an option where you go home and take a nap?"

"Nope."

"I didn't think so. I guess it couldn't hurt to head over to the shops on Second Street. And you're correct, Scooter does need new cleats. I should call Phyllis to let her know I won't be in today."

Zak had an office at Zimmerman Academy, the private school for gifted children we ran. Phyllis King was the school administrator.

"That's a good idea. While you have her on the phone, make sure she knows about Willa. I probably should have called her myself, but everything happened so quickly."

"I'm sure she must have heard, but I'll make sure," Zak promised. "Should I have her bring Alex home after classes?"

I thought about the list of ideas floating around in my head and knew that even though I'd promised to stay on the sidelines I wasn't going to be happy sitting at home. "Yes, that would probably be best. I'll call Tucker's aunt to see if she can drop Scooter at the house after school as well."

Tucker Willis was Scooter's best friend. After Scooter's dad decided to let Scooter remain in our care for the time being, he'd asked to enroll in the public middle school with Tucker rather than signing up to attend Zimmerman Academy with Alex, as he'd had initially wanted. Zak and I thought that the best choice as well because, although they were good friends and the same age, Alex was years ahead of Scooter academically.

"I need you to promise me something," Zak said after he hung up with Phyllis.

"What's that?"

"You need to promise me you won't go off sleuthing by yourself. I know you want to find Willa's killer, but you're carrying precious cargo and that has to take top priority."

I placed my hand on my stomach. "I know. I won't go off on my own, and if I have any leads that need to be explored I'll either call Salinger or be sure you're with me."

Zak didn't answer right away.

"Okay?" I asked.

There was a frown on his face, but he nodded.

"Great. Let's finish up this very nutritious meal and then head over to Second Street. I have a feeling we're going to come up with an important clue that will break this whole thing wide open."

Fortunately, or perhaps unfortunately, I was right.

The storefronts surrounding the Second Street Community Parking Lot were eclectic in nature. There were offices, like the ones of an accountant and a dentist; larger stores such as the sporting goods and hardware stores; and smaller local businesses such as a dress shop, a bakery, and a bookstore. I had no idea where Willa might have been going, so Zak and I decided to start on one side of the street, walk to the end, and then return along the opposite side.

Our first stop was the bookstore. There was only one person inside, entering data into a journal, when Zak and I entered, so we went directly to the counter.

"Can I help you?" the friendly-looking woman, who looked to be in her midthirties, asked.

"We're trying to trace the actions of a friend of ours who was in the neighborhood yesterday. We know she was around in the late afternoon and we wondered if you'd seen her."

"Is your friend missing?"

I paused as I debated how to answer. "Actually, she's dead." I handed the clerk a photo of Willa.

"That's the tax lady. She's dead?"

"I'm afraid so."

The woman frowned. "Yeah, I saw her. She came in to remind me that my local sales tax was late and I'd be penalized if it wasn't paid by the end of the month."

"Was she here alone?" I asked.

"Yeah, she was alone. She always comes alone."

"Does she often remind the local shopkeepers of late payments in person?"

The woman nodded. "Every darn quarter. You'd think the town would just send a late notice informing us of the due dates and accompanying penalties, but this lady was a real stickler for timely payments. It seemed like she got joy out of bullying people and threatening their livelihood if they didn't toe the line. I understand I owe the money, but it isn't always easy to come up with the cash right away. This is my slow season. I told her things would pick up after Thanksgiving and I would get caught up then, but she didn't seem to care that my business is seasonal. It was her opinion that I should have been setting money aside each month so I could pay the tax when it was due."

I found I had to agree with Willa's logic, but I didn't say as much. I picked up a book that was sitting on the counter and turned it over, pretending to look at the back. "I guess it made you mad that she was being so stringent."

The woman lifted one shoulder. "Yeah, I guess. I always pay my taxes, so I don't see what the big deal is if I'm a few weeks late. I guess someone with a government job and a regular income wouldn't understand how hard it is for small businesses to get by."

I set the book back on the counter along with a twenty-dollar bill. "Yeah. I guess it would be hard for someone with a regular income to understand the challenges of juggling bills when tourism drops off. Do you remember what time Willa was here?"

The woman rolled her eyes up into her head, as if searching for the answer. "I guess around four. Maybe a little after."

"So, she reminded you about your taxes. Then what?"

"I told her I'd send them in as soon as I could. She gave me a piece of paper that showed how much I owed and what the penalties were and left. I'm sure she was hitting up other businesses in the area."

I glanced at Zak, who had stood behind me and hadn't said a word. He nodded, and we said good-bye and left.

"I suppose the fact that she was debt collecting in the hours before she died could provide a motive," Zak commented as we walked to the barbershop next door.

"Yeah. Willa could be a force to reckon with when it came to things like local taxes. We were late paying the taxes for Zoe's Zoo one quarter, not because we didn't have the money but because we were busy and forgot all about filing the paperwork. Willa came by demanding immediate payment, even though we'd never been late before. She even charged us a ten percent penalty. And the worst part was, she acted like we were intentionally trying to cheat the town out of what was due it. As if!"

"If she treated you and Jeremy like that—people she knew, liked, and worked with—just imagine how she must treat business owners who are new to the area or really are trying to skate through for a couple of months."

I wrinkled my nose. "I guess I'm beginning to understand how she might have ended up dead."

Zak opened the door for me and we walked into the barbershop. Zak took the lead this time, but the barber indicated he hadn't seen Willa the previous day. By the time we made it to the end of the block and were preparing to turn around and start back down the opposite side, we had a good handle on what Willa was doing in the hours before her death.

"This is new," I said to Zak as we stood in front of a pet shop that was just around the corner from the Second Street shops.

"Just opened last week."

"How did I not know that? It should be my job to know about the pet shops in town."

"You've been busy with other things and Jeremy has been running things at the Zoo. I'm sure he must have mentioned it. You must have forgotten."

I frowned. "I guess." I looked in the front window. "If they just opened they wouldn't be behind on taxes, but there may have been new-business paperwork they failed to turn in. Given the fact that Willa was wrapped in a blanket with tons of dog hair, I think this might be a real possibility in terms of the scene of the murder. Let's just look around a bit, see if we see any blood or other physical evidence. I'll just say I heard they'd opened and wanted to introduce myself."

Zak opened the door. "Sounds good, but remember, keep it light and casual."

The shop sold a variety of pets and pet supplies, including puppies and kittens. Personally, I'm not a fan of pet stores selling animals. In my opinion, it encourages puppy and kitten mills, where the only point in reproduction is to make a quick buck. My purpose here today, however, wasn't to give the owner of the new store a lecture on a subject he clearly wasn't going to be interested in anyway. I held my tongue and instead headed down the aisle filled with cute dog toys.

"Can I help you find something?" a middle-aged man with faded blue eyes and a receding hairline asked.

I pasted on my most welcoming smile as I turned and faced the man. "Hi. My name is Zoe. I own Zoe's Zoo."

The man held out a hand. "I'm Mortie. I'm happy to meet someone in the same line of business as myself."

Hardly, I thought. Instead, I said, "It's nice to meet you as well. I guess I've been pretty busy lately. I didn't even know a pet store had opened up in town."

"It all happened pretty fast. I've always wanted to own a pet store and I was in Ashton Falls on vacation a while back when I saw this storefront for rent. I lined up some vendors, located some livestock, and here we are."

I cringed at the use of the word *livestock* for domesticated animals. "I'm surprised you were able to get a permit from the town so fast. It took me months."

The man leaned forward, lowered his voice, and said, "Between you and me, I didn't wait for the permit. I figured I could take care of all that after I got the place up and running. My brother did a similar thing in the town where he owns a business and it worked out fine. My brother's town wanted the sales tax income and was willing to let him stay open while he handled the paperwork, but apparently, the folks in Ashton Falls aren't as easy to work with. The witch who works for the town actually threatened to have me arrested if I didn't close my doors immediately. As if I could. I have a building full of animals to offload. Closing things down for a month or two would be the end of me before I even got started."

"Willa can be a stickler for the rules. I'm surprised she didn't send the sheriff over."

"She said she was going to, but I took care of things. Would you like a tour?"

I smiled. "I would."

Other than the fact that the store dealt with unlicensed breeders, I could see they might do well; they seemed to provide quality products when it came to their nonliving inventory. The dog food I bought for our family pets was cheaper here than it was at the feedstore. I supposed it could just be a loss leader to get folks in the door, but I wouldn't be at all surprised to find out that the owner of the feedstore was less than thrilled that he had a competitor in town after years of being the only supplier of quality pet food.

The floors, shelves, and cages were all spotlessly clean, which meant there wasn't any evidence to find, even if Willa had been in the shop when she died. I had pretty much decided we weren't going to discover anything of real value to our investigation until the shop owner brought us into the back, where the groomer he hired worked. Laying on the floor was a blanket with the exact design of the blanket used to cover Willa's body. Zak pinched me when I opened my mouth. I closed it and glared at him.

"We should get going, sweetie," Zak said, ushering me to the front door as fast as he could pull me along. "You know the kids will be waiting."

I tried to dig in my heels, but it was no use. Zak was a lot stronger than I was. "It was nice meeting you," I said over my shoulder as Zak forcefully pulled me out the door. Once we were safely outside I turned and looked at my very pushy husband. "What was that all about?"

"I had a feeling you were going to either ask the man about the blanket or confront him about killing Willa. Doing either is something best left to Salinger."

"I wasn't going to confront him."

Zak lifted one brow.

"I wasn't," I defended myself. "I might have asked about the blanket, but that was it."

Zak reached into my jeans pocket and pulled out my cell. He handed it to me. "Call Salinger."

I did as Zak said and we agreed to wait in the car and meet him when he arrived.

Chapter 5

Zak and I grabbed Scooter's cleats and headed home as soon as Salinger arrived. He was, after all, the cop and certainly didn't need our help to question the suspect. Salinger could see I was less than thrilled with being pushed out of things, but he agreed to call to fill us in after he sorted out exactly what had gone down.

"Do we need to grate more cheese?" I asked Zak as he assembled the lasagna we planned to serve that evening.

"No. It should be good. You might want to make a salad. I'm going to do garlic bread as well. What time did Ellie say they'd be over?"

"They should be here within a half hour," I answered. "She wanted to give Eli a bath before she changed her clothes. I guess he's become a bit of a splasher."

Zak set down the spoon he'd been holding and crossed the room. He pulled me into his arms. "I'm getting pretty excited to meet our own little splasher."

I smiled. "Yeah. Me too. I'll also be excited to have my body back. All the restrictions are getting real old real fast."

Zak kissed the tip of my nose. "Does that mean you don't want to have more children?"

"How about we have this one and see how it goes? I never realized how much I'd miss coffee, wine, sushi, and salami until I couldn't have it. Oh, and uninterrupted sleep and touching my toes."

"You can still touch your toes," Zak countered.

"Maybe, but I won't be able to for long."

Zak ran the back of his finger down the side of my cheek. "I know pregnancy has been hard on you so far. I'm sorry. I wish I could do all the hard parts for you."

I put my arms around Zak's waist and rested my head on his chest. "It's been fine. I don't even know why I'm complaining. Of course, I'll happily give up whatever I have to in order to have a healthy baby. Oh! After what happened I totally forgot to tell you that Ellie helped me come up with a theme and color scheme for the nursery."

Zak's arms tightened a bit around my body. "She did? That's wonderful. What are you thinking?"

I described the enchanted-woods theme and even outlined the mural I'd begun to imagine in my mind.

"I love it. I really do. We'll need to look for an artist to do the wall."

"Jeremy is a very talented artist as well as a musician. I thought I'd ask him to do the mural. Ellie is going to make a comforter for the crib and a pad for the changing table, and we'll go ahead and use the furniture your mom sent. Which just means we need to find a way for my mom to contribute, so no one will feel left out."

"Maybe she can help you pick out clothes for Catherine. Or a stroller. Or even a car seat. I guess we should make a list."

I laughed. "Yeah, I guess we should." I kissed Zak on the lips and took a step back. "I'm going to go up to check on the kids. Holler if the Dentons arrive."

One of the concerns I'd had when I found out Zak and I were going to have a biological child was that the nonbiological children we were raising would feel left out. We'd discussed the possibility and both of us had gone out of our way not only to make Alex and Scooter felt included but to make certain they knew that loving Catherine wouldn't cause us to love them any less.

"How's the homework going?" I asked Scooter as I poked my head in through his open bedroom door.

"Finished."

I walked into the room and sat down on the edge of his bed, next to his dog, Digger. "It seems like things might be a little easier this year."

He tilted his head as he drew a picture of a superhero on the pad in front of him. "They do seem easier, and I guess I'm trying harder. I want to do really good this year. As good as Alex."

I ran my hand through his longish hair. "I think that's an excellent goal. Did Zak give you the cleats we bought today?"

"Yup."

"Did you try them on?"

"Yup."

"Did they fit?"

"Nope."

My face fell. "No? Why not?"

"Too small."

"But we just had your feet measured a month ago."

"Guess they grew. Zak's going to exchange them tomorrow."

"At the rate you're growing, it won't be long before you're as tall as Zak."

Scooter looked up from his drawing. "Think so?"

"I do. Your dad is tall. I don't see any reason you won't be tall as well."

Scooter bowed his head and returned to his drawing, but not before I noticed a huge smile on his face. He adored Zak and wanted to be just like him when he grew up. He was working on his grades and had been spending time on the computer. Scooter didn't have the elevated IQ Zak and Alex did, but now that he was trying, I knew in my heart in the long run he was going to be fine.

I chatted with Scooter for a few minutes, then went to Alex's room. Her door was closed, so I knocked and she invited me to come in. She was sitting on the bed, bottle feeding one of the three kittens Jeremy had entrusted her with. Alex had a way with animals and loved to help, so somewhere along the way she'd become a temporary foster mom whenever we had a litter in need of special attention.

"It looks like they're growing," I said as I sat down on the corner of Alex's bed.

"They are. Jeremy said they've all gained weight and should grow into healthy adults."

"You've been so busy with school and your foster mothering, we haven't had time to get you a dress for the dance on Friday. How about we go shopping tomorrow after school but before Scooter's soccer game?"

Alex's smile faded. "It's okay. I don't need a dress. I decided not to go."

"Not go? But you were so excited about it."

Alex lifted one shoulder in a half-shrug. "I know, but I changed my mind. I think I'll just hang out here."

I was fairly certain Alex's not wanting to go to the dance translated into Alex's date bailing out on her.

"What happened?" I asked.

"Nothing happened. I just changed my mind."

"Did Mark bail out?"

Alex nodded. "But it's not his fault. He felt uncomfortable after Zak said they needed to have a talk before we went out."

"I see." Zak was a total sweetheart, and kids everywhere loved him, but he tended to be overly protective when it came to Alex. I knew part of the problem was that she'd initially entered high school when she was only twelve and her peers were fourteen to eighteen. She had no problem hanging with the older kids academically, but Zak did have a point that she wasn't necessarily up to par socially. Still, Alex was a smart girl and I felt we needed to trust her. Besides, she was thirteen now, and despite the fact that Mark was two years older, they were attending a dance chaperoned by both her surrogate parents. I really didn't see the need to give the poor boy the third degree. "If I could get Zak to agree to let you attend the dance with Mark minus the parental lecture, do you think Mark would reconsider?"

Alex lifted one shoulder. "I don't know. Maybe. He might have already asked someone else. I'm not really sure."

I tucked a lock of Alex's waist-length hair behind her ear. "I know Zak can go overboard when it comes to you dating, but it's only because he loves you so much and doesn't want anyone to hurt you."

"I know. I'm not mad."

"Let me talk to him. I really want you to go to the dance. I know Zak does as well."

"I talked to Eve," Alex said, referring to her best friend. "She said I shouldn't want to go to the dance with a boy who's too scared to talk to my dad."

"Do you agree with her?"

Alex shrugged. "I don't know. Maybe. But I do want to go to the dance and I do want to go with a date, and Mark is the only one who asked."

"Is Eve going?"

"Yeah. She invited me to go with her, but she's been seeing the same guy for a few months now. I didn't want to feel like a third wheel."

"I get that. Let me talk to Zak and you and I will talk about this again in the morning. Ellie, Levi, and Eli are coming for dinner, so get your kittens all fed, then wash up and come on down."

"Okay. I won't be long."

I was halfway to my own room to wash up when my phone rang. It was Salinger.

"Did you arrest the guy?" I asked as soon as I answered.

"No. He said he'd bagged up a whole load of blankets for the cleaners and had set it in the back of his open truck. He insisted someone must have stolen one of his soiled blankets from his laundry bag."

"That seems a little too convenient," I pointed out. "He admitted Willa was trying to have him shut down. He has a motive."

"He said he was in the store until after seven. I need to verify that, but if it's true I don't see how he would have had time to kill Willa and then dump her body over two miles away. Besides, I didn't find any evidence of blood on the premises. If he's our guy we'll need more."

Dang. I really thought we had the lowlife who killed Willa.

"Was there anyone else in the store who can verify the fact that he was there the whole time?" I asked.

"He says he was alone, but the clerks in the shops that border his might have seen or heard something. I'm following up."

"Okay. Keep me posted. I want to catch this guy as soon as possible."

Ellie and family had arrived by the time I made it back downstairs. Alex was playing with Eli in the den while Levi and Ellie were sitting at the kitchen counter chatting with Zak as he finished making our meal.

"Sounds like you've had a busy day," Ellie commented as I joined them at the counter.

"Not really. Zak and I did go to talk to the business owners around the Second Street parking lot, but it looks like our lead suspect might have petered out."

"Petered out?" Zak asked. "What happened?"

"I just spoke to Salinger. The owner of the pet store said he had a laundry bag filled with soiled blankets in the back of his open truck and insisted that if one of his blankets was used in Willa's murder someone must have stolen it from there."

"That doesn't sound right," Levi said.

"I agree. The problem is that Salinger didn't find any other physical evidence and the guy said he was at his store until after seven last night. Salinger's going to follow up, and in my book, he's still at the top of the suspect list. He seemed to have motive and his claiming the blanket Willa was wrapped in just happened to have been stolen from his laundry bag seems questionable."

"It also seems to indicate Willa was killed in that area," Levi pointed out. "Whether the blanket was one the pet shop owner took from his store after killing Willa or it was stolen by someone else who did, it makes sense it was used because it was convenient. I'm sure Salinger's looked around the entire Second Street area, but I'd pay particular attention to the area around the pet store."

"That's a good point," I said.

"Does Salinger have any other strong suspects?" Ellie asked.

"Not really. He has a list of names he's following up on, but no one stands out. It just seems to me that someone knows something and hasn't come forward, given the fact that Willa's body was dropped in a somewhat busy alley at the door of a popular restaurant during the dinner hour."

"It does seem there should have been one or more witnesses," Ellie agreed. "I don't have an additional suspect, but I may have eliminated one. I spoke to Henrietta today and she said she and the three hairdressers who work for her got a great deal on a space in Bryton Lake, so they're moving the whole business down the mountain. It sounds like a good opportunity and she didn't seem bitter about having to move. In fact, with the larger population in Bryton Lake, she has plans to take on a couple more stylists. We spoke for a good twenty minutes and at no point did I pick up the vibe that she was holding some huge grudge against Willa. I think we can take her off our list."

"Speaking of lists, maybe we should start one. After our conversation this morning I've had a mental list, but I never did commit it to paper." I slid off my barstool and crossed the room. I opened a drawer and took out a pen and a small pad of paper. "Okay, who do we have?"

"Cory Danielson," Levi jumped right in. "Your dad observed him having a loud argument with Willa, and Tawny reported they might have been dating because she'd seen Cory's car outside Willa's house. It's occurred to me that, more often than not, love is the motive for murder."

"That's grim," Ellie complained.

"Grim but true."

"Personally, I like Porky Walfer as a suspect," she added. "While Levi may have a point about the love connection, it's my opinion that money is usually the root of all evil. If Porky had to remove his deck he'd have been out a lot of money."

I wrote down Porky's name after Cory's. I also added the pet store owner I knew only as Mortie. I'd have to ask Salinger what his last name was. "Anyone else?"

"What about the fact that it was female skin under Willa's fingernails?" Zak asked. "All three of the current suspects are male."

"Good point." Levi nodded.

"Because we don't know for certain the killer and the person Willa scratched are the same person I don't think we should limit ourselves to female suspects, but Zak makes a good point," I admitted. "We need to widen our criteria. I'm sure there are dozens of people Willa pissed off in the past few weeks. She did have a way of getting under your skin. What about TJ? Salinger said the last entry on Willa's calendar was TJ at five o'clock. We know she was over on Second Street at that time. Maybe we should see if there are any business owners with those initials."

"Can you find a file of business owners online?" Ellie asked Zak.

"I can. After dinner. The lasagna is ready and I think it may very well be one of my best."

Chapter 6

After dinner Alex and Scooter settled into the den to watch a movie, Ellie put Eli to bed in the room we used as our guest nursery, and Levi and Zak headed to the computer room to begin the research on the suspects we'd identified so far. I took the five dogs in the house out for a quick walk along the deserted stretch of beach that bordered our home. It was a cold but clear night and the stars overhead seemed so close I felt I could almost touch them.

Levi and Ellie's dogs, Shep and Karloff, ran on ahead with Scooter's dog Digger, while Zak's Bella hung back with Charlie and me. Charlie seemed to be doing fine with all the additions to our ever-growing family, considering four years ago it had been just the two of us living in what was, at the time, my tiny boathouse. Still, I did worry that he might be jealous of Catherine when she arrived. I had plans to spend quality time with my little buddy after the baby was born in the hope that he'd take that new addition to the family as well as he'd taken the others. My cats, Marlow and Spade, had all but switched their alliance to Alex and rarely ventured into my room these days, so I wasn't overly concerned about the feelings of either being displaced when Catherine joined the family. Charlie was the only family pet attached to me above the others.

Charlie ran ahead a few steps and began digging in the sand. I paused to wait for him because he wasn't the sort of dog who randomly dug holes. After he'd dug down four or five inches he grabbed something with his mouth and brought it to me. Charlie dropped a delicate necklace with a golden M on it into my outstretched hand. The necklace wasn't mine, but it might belong to my mother, whose name was Madison. I supposed it was possible she might have dropped it while visiting, which she did more and more frequently since I'd become pregnant.

"I guess we should head back," I said to the dogs, who all changed direction and started back toward the house. I loved these solitary walks after dark and wondered how being the mother of an infant would affect my ability to slip away whenever the urge for peace and quiet overtook me. I was both excited and worried about being a mother. Mostly, I was excited to hold my new baby in my arms and watch her grow into a young woman who would eventually marry and provide me with grandbabies I could hold in my arms. But there was a part of me that whispered in my ear during quiet moments such as this that my life would no longer be my own. Marrying had changed my life, and deciding to raise Alex and Scooter had changed it even more. But a baby? A baby would require the biggest change of all. I just hoped I was up for everything life had to throw at me because in my heart I knew Catherine deserved a mother who would have the right answers in any situation and, most importantly, would always be there for her, no matter where her journey took her.

Back in the house, I made sure the dogs all had water and then headed for the den, where Zak, Levi, and Ellie were waiting for me.

"So catch me up," I said after grabbing my pad and pen and taking a seat on the sofa.

Zak turned back to his computer, where he pulled up an official-looking document on the screen. He scrolled down a bit and then began to speak. "So far I pulled the town files on all the businesses within one square block of the Second Street parking area. There are fourteen businesses in this small area, not including the larger box stores, of which there are three. The taxes for the box stores are paid by their corporate offices, so it seems unlikely Willa would have visited them even if they were late on their payments. I focused exclusively on the small businesses. Nine of them are owned by men and five by women. None of the business owners have names that correspond to the initials TJ."

"Can you tell how many of the fourteen are behind in their tax payments?" I asked.

"Three. The bookstore we visited today is owned by a woman named Darla Medford. She appears to have a history of late payments to the county. There were quite a few references to meetings, letters, and phone calls on Willa's part over the past several years. There was even a mention on file of an altercation last winter that led to the barber next door calling the cops to break it up."

"Wow. That sounds pretty serious. Was it a physical altercation?"

"Based on what's in the file, it looks as if Ms. Medford verbally assaulted Willa. There's a mention of her threatening Willa with some sort of unspecified payback if she didn't back off and learn to be a bit more flexible. In this case I'm going to suggest we call Salinger to see what he can add to the information in the file. Chances are he was the one who responded to the call."

I jotted Darla Medford's name down on my list. "I'll call him in the morning. Who else do we have?"

"Bruce Rice owns a ski and ski equipment rental and repair shop in the winter and bicycles, paddleboards, and boating equipment in the summer. He seems to have mostly a good record in terms of paying his local taxes on time, but he did miss the payment that was due on October 15. It would have been only a few days late, so I doubt Willa would have made too much of an issue about it, but if she was in the area for another reason she may very well have stopped in."

"And it's possible Mr. Rice didn't take kindly to Willa's oftentimes brusque approach to her job," I finished. "I'll add him to the list."

"The final business within this one-block radius that was late with its tax payment is the secondhand store owned by Matilda Presley. Ms. Presley is over six months late with her payments and, according to the file, Willa was in the process of having her business shut down."

"Sounds like she had motive to want Willa out of the way. I'll add her to the list. Anyone else stand out?"

"Other than Mortie Sawyer from the pet shop, not really," Zak answered.

"Maybe we should go window-shopping tomorrow," I suggested. "While we're out we can look for business owners or even employees with scratch marks on their faces. Because Willa's car was found in the nearby parking area it seems to me whatever went down occurred in that vicinity."

"Sounds fine to me," Zak said.

"I agree the murder most likely occurred in that area," Ellie joined in, "but we should keep in mind that it's possible Willa met someone while there and left with them for some reason. Maybe she had a date or was going to have dinner with a friend. Or maybe she was grabbed while entering or leaving her car and driven to another location. In any case, the physical evidence could be somewhere else entirely."

"If that happened how did she end up wrapped in one of the pet store blankets?" I asked.

"Oh, yeah, I forgot about that. I guess she must have been killed there. I guess that does help us to focus in."

"I think even if we can find the actual crime scene, this is going to be a tough case," Levi stated.

"Aren't they all?" I asked.

Levi nodded. "Yeah, I guess. I'm afraid I'm not going to be a lot of help. I have classes every day this week and football practice every afternoon. We have an away game on Friday, so I need to be sure the boys are ready. And we have the Hamlet this weekend. With the exception of offering an opinion or verbal support, I'm going to have to sit this one out."

"I'm pretty busy this week as well," Zak offered. "But I don't want Zoe going out sleuthing alone and I know she won't be content to sit this one out, so I'll make the time. Let's chat with Salinger in the morning, then decide what to do next."

Zak logged off his computer and turned in his chair. "Who wants dessert?"

******

Once the Denton family left and I got Alex and Scooter tucked into bed, I went upstairs with Charlie to wash up. Zak was in his office, and it looked like he was working on a project Zimmerman Software had contracted to do. I really did feel bad for him. Not only did he have his software business to stay on top of but he had Zimmerman Academy to run and the kids to parent. I hated that he felt he had to take time out of his busy schedule to babysit me. Maybe I really should take a step back and let Salinger handle things on his own. I knew Zak would be relieved if I came to that decision.

I changed out of my jeans and sweater and into a pair of soft gym shorts and a baggy long-sleeved T-shirt. I had a drawer full of sexy nightwear, but lately I hadn't been feeling sexy at all. I didn't want to bother Zak, so I tried to read, but my mind kept wandering. I opened the nightstand drawer, pulled out the remote, and clicked on the television. There were a couple of spooky movies on that I usually enjoyed at Halloween, but after the real-life horror I'd witnessed the previous evening I found I didn't quite have the stomach for blood and gore.

I clicked off the television and instead grabbed my notebook. So far, we'd identified seven suspects: Porky Waller, Cory Danielson, Mortie Sawyer, Darla Medford, Bruce Rice, Matilda Presley, and TJ, whoever that might be. All seemed to have motives, except for TJ, who was unidentified as yet, but even I had to admit it would be a long shot if Willa was killed over a conflict resulting from overdue taxes. Ellie had said she'd pretty much eliminated Henrietta Toffer as a suspect, so she'd never made the written list.

It appeared Willa had died from blunt force trauma to the head. With that sort of injury, the attack was more likely a crime of passion or even a simple accident. It was possible Willa had had an argument with someone that had resulted in the killer grabbing a nearby object and hitting her with it, or perhaps even pushing her, leading to a fall in which she'd hit her head.

The big question in my mind was why Rosie's? If Willa was on Second Street making collection calls, resulting in an altercation that led to her death, why would the killer wrap her in a blanket and drop her at Rosie's back door? Why not bury her somewhere out of town or drop her in the lake? If you were going to go to all the trouble to move the body, why not dump it in an isolated part of the woods or in the next county? The fact that she was dumped at Rosie's had to be a clue, but so far, I had no idea what that clue was.

Ellie and I had gone to dinner at Rosie's on the spur of the moment. We hadn't planned it or told anyone what we were doing, so I knew the placement of Willa's body couldn't have been in any way a jab at me, the way last year's cryptic notes had been. Rosie's had sold twice since Rosie herself had owned it and Ellie had worked there. The current owner was a man who lived in Boston and had bought the restaurant as an investment. I'd never met him, but I'd heard he was the son of a rich and powerful man, Anthony Bianchi, who, if rumor could be believed, at one time had been linked to the mob. After Anthony Bianchi Senior died his son had taken over the family business. From what I knew, the family owned restaurants and other small businesses across the country.

Rosie's new manager was a woman named Ginger Messenger. I didn't know her well, but Ellie had made a point of introducing herself when she first started and she'd in turn introduced me. I knew Willa had met her as well because the events committee met in Rosie's backroom every Tuesday morning, and Willa had worked it out for us to continue to use the room even after the business sold.

The food at Rosie's was as good as it had ever been, but the overall ambience had changed with the new ownership. Rosie had sold to an individual who was interested in running the business herself, but she'd then sold to the Bianchis, who were more interested in the bottom line than the hometown atmosphere. Quite a few of the employees had quit, and several longtime patrons had stopped coming in once the new management was in place, but the service was still decent and the employees seemed friendly, so as far as I was concerned it was still a very good place to eat.

I did have to wonder, however, if the placement of Willa's body hadn't had something to do with the restaurant's new ownership. Could Willa, being Willa, have had an altercation with Mr. Bianchi who, as far as I could tell, was a lot more powerful and sophisticated than the small-time business owners Willa was used to pushing around? In my mind, a man who ran a large family business probably wouldn't be cowed by Willa's bullying. I also knew Willa wasn't the sort to stand down, so an altercation of one variety or the other seemed to be inevitable given enough time. Had Bianchi hired someone to eliminate Willa and had the contract killer then delivered the package? I guessed that was a bit of a long shot and not a smart move on Bianchi's part if that were what had happened.

"I didn't know you were still up," Zak said as he walked through the bedroom door.

"I wouldn't have gone to sleep without saying good night. Did you get your program finished?"

"I did my part and forwarded it to Pi. He'll do his thing and then send it back."

Pi was Zak's ward, Peter Irwin, who was not only attending college but training to be Zak's business partner as well. Pi was an intelligent young man who had a knack for anything having to do with technology and was almost as good a hacker as Zak. Alex also wanted to work with Zak one day, but I had a feeling her parents, who were both archaeologists, might have other ideas.

"Did you check to see if the front door was locked?" I asked. "I forgot to when I came in."

"I checked it. Give me a minute to wash up and I'll join you."

I watched Zak enter the adjoining bathroom and wondered if this might not be a good time to talk to him about Alex and the dance. I sort of hated to bring it up just before bed, but we both had a busy week and I hoped if I could convince Zak to back off, Mark would reconsider and go with Alex as planned.

Charlie must have realized he was about to lose his place next to me because he snuggled into my side as tightly as he could before resting his head on my stomach. I put my arm around my little buddy and caressed his soft fur. Maybe Charlie was feeling a bit displaced with all the changes after all.

When Zak returned he smiled at Charlie and made sure to leave him plenty of room. He reached a foot over to mine so that at least that part of our bodies was touching, even if the rest of us had a furry white dog between us.

"Are you ready to turn off the light or do you want to talk or watch some television?" Zak asked.

"Actually, I do want to talk to you. It's about Alex."

"And what's going on with Alex?"

"She told me this evening that she isn't going to the dance. Mark backed out after you made a big deal about having a talk with him before their date."

Zak frowned. "I take it by your tone of voice that you don't approve? Isn't that what parents of sweet, innocent little girls are supposed to do? Vet the hormone-driven boy who wants to get them alone in their car?"

I couldn't help laughing. "Zak, you really need to lighten up. First, Alex might be young, but she's sophisticated and intelligent and, most importantly, she can take care of herself. Additionally, Mark doesn't drive yet. He's only fifteen. We were going to give the kids a ride to the dance with us. And then there's the fact that Mark is one of your students and in no way a stranger. I know you like him. And last, the dance is at the school and will be well chaperoned. I don't think you have a thing to worry about."

"If there's nothing to worry about why is Mark scared to talk to me?"

"Because he's a socially awkward fifteen-year-old and you're a six-and-a-half-foot-tall millionaire with a reputation for being overprotective."

Zak paused, then nodded. "Okay. I guess you have a point. I'll talk to Mark tomorrow to let him know it's okay to take Alex to the dance."

"I think it will be better to let Alex handle her own dating life. Why don't you tell her at breakfast that for this one time only you're waiving the requirement of an interview with Daddy Warbucks and let her decide whether to tell Mark."

Zak picked up my hand and kissed my palm. "Okay. Whatever you think is best. But in the future, we meet the boy before the date."

"Fine."

Zak turned off the light and lay on his side. It was obvious Charlie wasn't moving tonight, so we cuddled around him as he snuggled up in the middle.

Chapter 7

Wednesday, October 25

Catherine seemed to want to get up at the crack of dawn, so I bundled up, grabbed the three dogs, and headed out for a walk along the beach. The sun had yet to rise above the mountain, so it was still cold out, but I felt a restless energy I couldn't quite quell and hoped the walk would help. Charlie stayed right next to my side, but the other two ran ahead.

"So, what's going on, little guy?" I asked my furry best friend. "It seems you're feeling insecure, but nothing out of the ordinary has occurred and Catherine isn't even born yet, so it can't be that. Are you feeling okay?"

Charlie looked up at me with his huge brown eyes. My heart melted a bit, but he looked healthy, so I didn't think he was physically ill. Maybe I'd been tense with everything that had been going on and he could sense it. He always had been hypersensitive to my moods. I suppose I could have interpreted his need to provide comfort *to* me as his need to seek comfort *from* me. I decided not to dwell on it but simply enjoy this quiet time with my little guy.

I loved my life. I really did. But even now, there were times I'd look back to the simplicity of my life when Charlie, Marlow, Spade, and I all lived in my tiny boathouse overlooking the lake. I'd worked for the county and spent evenings and weekends with best friends Levi and Ellie. I hadn't even known Salinger yet and certainly had never been involved in a dangerous murder investigation. My mom wasn't in the picture then, so it was just Dad, Grandpa, and me. Life had seemed perfect, and while I would never in a million years trade what I have now for what I had then, that didn't mean I didn't look back on the past with bittersweet longing for a time when life had been simpler.

I decided to head back to get started on breakfast. I had to admit that one of the things I missed most of all the things I'd given up for Catherine's sake was coffee. Before becoming pregnant I was a three-cup-per-morning person, so going cold turkey had been a bit of an adjustment. Still, no matter what I had to do, my baby was worth it, so I'd suck it up for a few more months even if it meant I had to walk around in a daze until my body adjusted.

I paused at the back door to remove my shoes, which were damp and sandy. I glanced in the kitchen window in time to see Alex hug Zak before trotting out the door to get ready for school. I smiled. He must have spoken to her as we'd discussed. He really was a very good father.

I picked up my shoes and left them near the bench in the mudroom and continued into the kitchen. "Something smells good."

"I'm making pumpkin nut muffins to go with the cheesy baked eggs I have in the oven. It's a perfect fall morning and I felt like indulging."

I stood on tiptoe and kissed Zak on the lips. They felt warm against my cold ones. The kitchen not only smelled wonderful with the scent of pumpkin and nutmeg but Zak had built a fire in the kitchen fireplace, giving the room a warm, cozy feel overall.

"I'm going to run up to take a quick shower. Don't let the kids eat all the muffins before I get back."

"I'll snag you a couple and set them aside."

After I'd taken a warm shower I dressed in a pair of yoga pants and an oversized sweatshirt. My jeans were to the point where I could barely zip them up and I hadn't gotten around to buying maternity clothes yet. I was leaning toward skipping the maternity garb altogether and hanging out in sweatpants until Catherine was born. My mom had been bugging me to take a day trip off the mountain to buy some cute new clothes, but it seemed like sort of a waste to spend all that money on clothes I'd only wear a short time. Of course Mom had a lot of money and so did Zak, so I supposed finances shouldn't be my primary reason not to make the trip. If I were being honest, the real reason I didn't want to go was because I hated shopping for clothes even when I wasn't feeling fat and bloated.

I grabbed my phone before leaving the bedroom, which was when I noticed a missed call from Salinger. Even though I was right upstairs, I decided to save myself a trip down the stairs to inform Zak I'd be a few more minutes and texted him instead. Once I got the thumbs-up reply I sat down on the edge of the bed and returned Salinger's call.

"Please tell me you've found Willa's killer." I'd immediately said what was in my mind the best-case scenario.

"I'm afraid not, but I do have some news. First, on the suspect front, you'd initially given me Cory Danielson's name and I spoke to him. I don't think he's our guy."

I remembered my dad had witnessed a fight between Willa and Cory outside of Donovan's last week, and Tawny thought they may have been dating.

"Did he say what the fight was about?"

"Cory didn't have the cash to renew his business license, so he worked out a deal with Willa."

"What sort of deal?" Cory was a contractor.

"She hired him to do some work at her house, which is why his car was seen there. In exchange, she was supposed to give him the cash he needed to renew his license. The fight was because Willa was a perfectionist Cory found impossible to deal with."

"Sounds about right." I crossed one leg over the other. "Okay, so why do you think he's innocent? Maybe Willa threatened not to pay him or even to sue him over what she considered to be shoddy workmanship."

"I know he's innocent because he's been working on a job in Bryton Lake since last Saturday. I called the customer and verified he was there until after eight o'clock on Monday night."

"Oh. I guess that's a pretty good alibi." Charlie trotted into the room through the open door and jumped up onto the bed. "Do you have any other news?"

"I may have a lead on the identity of TJ from the desk calendar. There's a bar over on Third Street called Tommy Joe's. If Willa was going to TJ's, and only to TJ's, there would have been closer places to park than the Second Street public lot, but if she was also going to do some tax collecting it's possible she parked on Second, made her stops, and then headed over to her five o'clock appointment. The bar doesn't open until two, but I plan to stop by this afternoon to see what I can find out."

"I thought the bar on Third was called Rockets."

"It was, but it sold last month. I'm not sure the TJ on the calendar was referring to Tommy Joe's, but so far, it's the only lead I have. You didn't manage to dig up anything, did you?"

Charlie put his head in my lap and I began to rhythmically scratch it. "Not in relation to the initials TJ, but we did find a couple of people in the area who were late with their taxes. Zak and I were going to go back later to rattle a few cages."

"Okay. Give me a call if you find anything or need backup."

"We will."

"And Zoe, be careful. I'd hate to see anything happen to either you or your baby."

"All we're going to do is talk to people," I promised.

******

After breakfast I ran the kids to school while Zak took care of some work he needed to do before we could head out sleuthing. Phyllis King, Zimmerman Academy's administrator, was standing in front of the school, greeting the students as they arrived, so I parked and head over to speak to her for a moment. Phyllis, like myself, had known Willa a long time, and I wanted to check in with her to see how she was doing.

"Zoe, how are you, dear?" She opened her arms and wrapped me in a hug. The Phyllis I used to know was never a hugger, but two years ago she'd opened her home to a group of Zimmerman Academy students and that seemed to have made all the difference.

"I'm fine, considering."

Phyllis lowered her head. "I heard what happened to Willa. I'm having such a hard time coming to terms with it. Willa could be rigid, but she was a nice woman and I'm going to miss her. Have you heard about a service?"

I shook my head. "No. I'm not even certain who her next of kin might be. I guess Salinger is looking in to it. I should ask him."

"I believe she had a sister in Boston." Phyllis narrowed her gaze. "Wanda. I believe her name was Wanda. I know she has a daughter, so I imagine she is or at least was married, which would mean she would have a different last name. I'm sure Salinger can find something if he looks for a Wanda Walton in Boston. It's possible she might not have married, or she may have married and kept her maiden name. Even if she changed it, you could probably track her down using Walton; maiden names do tend to stick."

"I'll be sure to tell him. And thank you for the information."

"Please let me know what you find out. If they have local services I'd like to pay my respects."

"I'll call you. Will you be at the dance on Friday?"

"I will and am very much looking forward to it. The kids seem excited as well. It'll be the first event in our new gym. I understand Alex is going with Mark."

I paused. "Maybe. I'm afraid Zak might have scared him away, but I spoke to him and he spoke to Alex, so I'm hoping things will work themselves out."

"Mark is a nice boy, but he is painfully shy," Phyllis said. "Alex is so sweet and such a patient soul. I think she'll be good for Mark. He needs someone to urge him out of his shell. I'll check in with Alex later and maybe give her a nudge in the right direction if I have to. There is no doubt in my mind that Alex will grow up to do great things with a man worthy of her love beside her, but when you are just thirteen, a boy who can be a friend and isn't interested in more really is the best choice."

"I agree. And thank you again."

I was headed toward home when the alarm on my phone started beeping and I suddenly remembered I'd set it so I wouldn't miss the county's inspection at the Zoo. I quickly changed direction toward the shelter. Jeremy was there and would be handling things, but I owned the facility and felt I should have a presence as well. I parked just as the inspector was entering the building. I took a minute to call Zak to tell him what I was doing, then followed the inspector inside.

"Zoe, I wasn't sure you'd be in."

"I wanted to be here just in case there were questions I could answer. You know how important this expansion is to me."

"I'm glad you're here. This is Milton Gordon. Mr. Gordon, this is the owner of Zoe's Zoo, Zoe Donovan-Zimmerman."

We shook hands and exchanged pleasantries, then I took a step back and let Jeremy take charge of the tour. The reality was, he had been the mastermind behind the expansion while I'd simply approved and paid for things. I missed spending time at the Zoo, but on most days of the week I was torn in a million directions. I still came in several mornings a week, mostly just to catch up with my staff and play with the animals, but there was no doubt in my mind that Jeremy could completely run things on his own if he had to.

I stopped off in my office and looked at the pile of mail waiting to be opened. I really did need to spend one morning here this week. I picked up the pile and began sorting through. A lot of what we received was junk mail from people wanting to sell us equipment and supplies, but important things sometimes crossed my desk. I was sure I would be spending a significant amount of time at the Zoo once Mother Zimmerman arrived for her much-dreaded visit, but when Catherine was born I'd have to turn over mail-opening duties to Jeremy, the way I'd slowly turned over everything else.

I was near the end of the pile when I noticed an envelope that had been addressed in crayon. It had my name on it and the correct address, but it looked as if a first grader had filled in the information. I opened the envelope and pulled out a single sheet of paper. There was a hand-dawn picture of a little girl with long dark hair holding an orange and white cat. At the top of the page was the word *application*. It was crudely written and the *p*'s were backward, so I had to assume the child who'd sent the picture to me had asked someone how to spell the difficult word. I wasn't sure who the child was, or how to get hold of her because there wasn't a return address on the envelope, but I figured Jeremy might know. I'd ask him when he was finished with the inspector, who I could hear Jeremy speaking to in the lobby. I should go out to see how the inspection had gone. We really needed to get the clearance today. If there were items to fix before we could receive the permit to open the new wing we'd have to decline the bear cubs we'd already said we would take for the winter.

"So, how was everything?" I asked with as much confidence as I could gather.

"Everything looks good," Mr. Gordon said. "I was just telling your manager how much I admire what you do here. I have a nephew who'd love to come to see the bears if you think a tour could be arranged."

"Anytime. Just call ahead so we're certain there's someone available to walk you through."

I blew out a breath of relief after the man handed me a temporary permit and assured me I would be getting final clearance in the mail. He assured me it was fine to go ahead and use the new wing as soon as we wanted, so I told Jeremy to call the rescue center to tell them it was fine to send over the cubs.

"I'll call them now."

"Before you do, do you recognize this?" I handed Jeremy the envelope in which the letter had come.

"It came with the mail on Friday."

"This was inside." I handed him the drawing. "Do you have any idea who sent it?"

"Hillary Wasserman."

"And who is Hillary Wasserman?" I asked.

"The first-grade class from the elementary school came by for a tour last week. There was a little girl with long dark hair and the biggest brown eyes I'd ever seen. When we went through the cat room she absolutely fell in love with the orange and white kitten. She wanted to take her home right then and there, but I told her that we only adopted our dogs and cats out to people who had filled out an application. It looks like she did just that."

"Aw." I felt my heart soften toward the child. "Do you know where she lives? Maybe I can stop by to talk to her parents. Do we still have the kitten?"

"We do have the kitten and I can look up her address. She really was a sweetie. I hope for her sake and the kitten's it works out."

Chapter 8

Zak had completed his work by the time I arrived back at the house. I'd stopped by Hillary's home and chatted with her mother, who seemed open to the idea of adopting the kitten, although she needed to speak to her husband first. I gave her an application as well as a business card and told her to get hold of either Jeremy or me when they'd made a decision. In the meantime, I told her I'd have Jeremy hold the kitten for a few days so they could discuss it.

Zak hadn't had a chance to see to the dogs, so we took them out for a quick walk and then set off to town. We needed to pick the kids up from school today so they had time to do their homework before Scooter's soccer game, so we only had a few hours to sleuth. I decided that narrowing down the suspect list was my main priority. I still thought Mortie from the pet store was our best suspect, but I wasn't sure what we could do that Salinger hadn't already done, so while I kept him at the top of the list, I decided to focus on those we hadn't yet spoken to.

Bruce Rice, the man who owned the sports rental and repair shop, confirmed that Willa had been by on Monday afternoon, but only to drop off a late notice. He'd assured her he would be paid up by the end of the month and she'd left after only a couple of minutes. He didn't seem to be lying and he *was* only a few days late, so I concluded his conversation with Willa hadn't ended in an altercation. Still, it wouldn't hurt to take a look around. The store was undergoing a transition from bikes and summer rental items to skis, snowboards, and equipment associated with the winter activities in the area. I found a pair of ski boots in Scooter's size and wondered if it wouldn't be best to buy used boots given the rate his feet were growing. The boots were in good shape, so I asked Bruce about them and he informed me that he sold his rental equipment after only one season, so most of his merchandise was still in excellent condition.

Zak engaged Bruce in a conversation about the advancements that had been made to snowboards in the past couple of years while I went on to look at the snowshoes. I was about to suggest to Zak that we be on our way when I noticed a tag with Willa's name on it laying on the floor. I picked it up and returned to where Zak and Bruce were chatting.

"I found this on the floor over near the snowshoes and ice skates," I said, handing Bruce the tag.

"Thanks. I must have dropped it. Ms. Walton asked me to put a pair of ice skates on hold for her when she was in on Monday, but when I heard she died I realized she wouldn't be back for the skates, so I returned them to stock."

I couldn't for the life of me imagine Willa ice skating, but she may have wanted to buy the skates for someone else. Nothing Bruce said or did had indicated to me that he was hiding anything, so I thanked him and hinted to Zak that we needed to move on to our next stop.

The first thing I noticed when I walked into the secondhand store owned by

Matilda Presley was the huge scratch on her cheek.

"Ouch! That looks like it hurts," I said as evenly as I could, trying desperately not to jump across the counter and tackle Willa's killer to the floor.

Matilda put her hand to her cheek. "It does. I guess it's my own fault for getting into a scuffle with someone who fights dirty."

"What happened?" I asked, hoping my expression conveyed sympathy. I glanced at Zak, who was frowning but hadn't said anything yet.

"My neighbor and I got into it over the fact that her dog spends most of its waking hours barking. The woman doesn't seem to care and does nothing to control the noise, even when he's barking for hours on end in the middle of the night. When the dog woke me up at four a.m. yesterday morning I'd had as much of the racket as I was going to take. I went stomping over to her house, where I proceeded to bang on her door. She answered with the dog in her arms and I lost it. I threatened to set out poison traps if she didn't put a muzzle on the beast and she slapped me."

"It looks like more than a slap."

"My neighbor has long nails that are more like talons."

"I see. You wouldn't really poison the dog, would you?"

"If she can't find a way to shut it up, you bet I will. Do you have any idea how annoying it is to be woken up four or five times a night every night?"

"I imagine it must be very annoying, but you don't have to kill the dog." I took a card from my pocket. "If you file a complaint there's a process we go through. If the issue isn't resolved the dog is removed from the home."

The woman took the card. "I'm happy to hear that."

"If you want to give me your neighbor's address I'll stop by to speak to her today. Maybe we can find a solution that will meet everyone's needs."

"Thanks, but I'll talk to her myself. Did you need help finding something?"

"Actually, I wanted to ask about a woman who may have been in here on Monday. Her name was Willa Walton and she worked for the town."

"She was in. I heard she died. I don't mean to sound harsh, but I can't say as I'm unhappy about the news. She was planning to shut me down because I got behind on my taxes. I tried to reason with her, maybe work out a payment plan, but she wouldn't budge. All I can say is, when the town hires a replacement I hope they find someone who's a little less rigid, a little more understanding."

"Seems like there are several business owners who had something similar to say about her."

Matilda shrugged. "We're all in the same boat. It's not easy making a living in this town. I've considered moving on more than one occasion, but at the end of the day I really enjoy living in the mountains. Was there something I could help you find?"

"My husband and I are just browsing today. I hope that's okay?"

"Knock yourself out."

Zak and I walked around the shop pretending to look at the merchandise while I was really looking for a sign that Willa had been killed in the shop. I planned to call Salinger to inform him about the scratch on Matilda's face as soon as I'd looked around a bit. I was hoping to find blood residue or some other indicator that Willa had been killed here, but nothing jumped out at me as suspicious. I nodded at Zak that we could leave. He took my arm and we headed to the door.

Outside, I called Salinger, who promised to follow up with Matilda. He agreed with me that the story about the fight with the neighbor seemed suspect given the situation and promised to look in to it. When I'd completed my call I turned to Zak and asked him where he wanted to head next.

He glanced at his watch. "We have time for one more stop. Any preferences?"

I thought about the suspects we had and the information we'd managed to gather. "Something odd is clearly going on with the shopkeepers around here; I'm just not sure exactly what. First Mortie just happened to have owned the blanket Willa's body was found wrapped in and then Matilda was scratched by a neighbor the morning after Willa scratched her attacker. Everything's a bit too convenient. Still, I'm not sure we'll get anything more out of either Matilda or Mortie without additional evidence to confront them with. The hardware store where Porky works is just down the street. Let's stop by there to see what he has to say. We can look at paint samples for the nursery while we're there. Jeremy's going to take care of the paint for the mural, but we'll need to decide what to use for the other walls."

Zak took my hand in his. "I'd like that. Let's go."

The short drive to the hardware store gave me a few minutes to gather my thoughts. It almost seemed as if Willa's murder had been carried out by multiple people. Could it be possible Matilda and Mortie were in on the attack together? Of course, even if they were, that still didn't explain where Willa had been killed and why her body had been dumped at Rosie's, of all places.

Porky was with a customer when we first arrived, so Zak and I went to the paint section. When Ellie had suggested using light blue to mimic the sky I'd thought that was a good idea, but who knew there were so many shades of blue?

I held up several sample cards and tried to decide what the differences were. "This one seems to have more of a purple base, whereas this one seems to be a bit greener. I like the pallet with the grayish tint, but I don't want anything too dark."

"What about his one?" Zak held up a card. "It's called bluebell. It's a little darker than the one called iceberg but not too dark."

I tried to picture it on the wall. "I know I said I liked the shades with a gray base, but I think this might be too gray. What about this one?"

"I think when you get it on the wall the purple undertones will really come through. We could use a slightly darker color, then trim the ceiling with a white crown molding."

"That would look nice," I agreed just as Porky walked over and asked if we needed help. I explained what we were looking for and he made a few suggestions, pointing out some subtle differences between the color families I hadn't noticed. Zak asked about paint brands while I tried to figure out how to bring Willa into the conversation.

"I should probably restain the deck before the snow hits," Zak said, which at least got the subject onto decks.

"It's good to do it every year," Porky confirmed. "I have a new brand of waterproof sealer that's gotten great reviews from everyone who's tried it. I used it on my own deck and so far, I really like it."

"I heard about the problems you've been having with your deck. Are you going to need to tear it down?" I asked.

"Not anymore." Porky grinned.

"That's good," I responded. "It would have been such a shame to lose it after all the expense you must have put into it. Did the town change the ordinance?"

"No, but the lady who was hell-bent on enforcing it is no longer in the picture."

"You must be referring to Willa," I said.

"I know the two of you worked together on the events committee and whatnot, and I'm sorry she died, but that woman was a thorn in my side. A lot of folks don't bother with permits, so it seemed unfair she was singling me out for harassment."

"It does seem unfair," I said. "Why do you think she was picking on you?"

"She was having some work done on her house and asked for a discount. I turned her down, and she must not have taken kindly to that because the next day she was out at my place to deliver a notice that my illegally built deck would need to be removed immediately."

I frowned. It didn't seem like Willa to ask for a discount, and while she was a stickler for the rules, I'd always known her to be professional, so Porky's assertion didn't really fit. Still, she *had* been working on her house, so maybe Porky was telling the truth. I wondered how I could find out for certain.

"And you don't think the person who replaces Willa is going to have the same issue with your deck?"

Porky shrugged. "I have a feeling by the time the town gets around to hiring a replacement my deck will be old news. You know how long it takes to hire government workers."

Porky had a point. It was a lengthy process, and whoever was hired would have a lot of catching up to do. His deck might very well be forgotten in the chaos.

After Zak and I left the hardware store we headed to the sporting goods store to exchange the cleats and then to the middle school to pick up Scooter. I wasn't sure the day had worked out the way I'd hoped. I'd wanted to begin eliminating suspects, but except for Bruce Rice, the suspects we'd interviewed stood out as being even stronger ones than I'd first imagined.

"I think Porky, Mortie, and Matilda definitely need to stay on the list," I said as Zak drove.

"I agree."

"What about Bruce? I didn't pick up on anything that would suggest he's the killer."

"I agree with that as well," Zak said. "What about Darla at the bookstore?"

"She wasn't a fan of Willa, but I don't consider her a strong suspect. I guess we can keep her toward the bottom of the list. The thing that doesn't fit with any of our current suspects is, why Rosie's?"

Zak turned into the parking lot of the middle school and got in line behind the other parents waiting to pick up their children. "It does seem like an odd place to dump a body," Zak said. "It's so odd, in fact, that I almost think answering that question will help us understand the rest."

"I wonder if we should interview the staff at Rosie's. Maybe someone knows something we don't."

"It'd have to be tomorrow. I'm afraid the remainder of our afternoon is going to be booked. Although…" Zak paused.

"Although what?" I asked.

"Tommy Striker's mom, Maria, works at Rosie's. He's going to start the game at left forward, so I'm sure she'll be there. It wouldn't hurt to strike up a conversation to see if she volunteers anything."

"That's a good idea. Not only does she work in the kitchen, where I happen to know a lot of gossip occurs among all the staff, but she worked for both the previous owner and the new one. I've been thinking that the new owner, a man named Anthony Bianchi, might somehow be involved in this whole thing. If there was something going on between Willa and Bianchi, Maria might know the details. And even if she doesn't know of a problem Maria might have seen or heard something on the night Willa's body was dumped. I know she was on shift because I remember seeing her there."

Chapter 9

I found I was excited to attend Scooter's soccer game. He was one of the best kids on the team, which meant he got a lot of playing time. Sports were his strength, where academia was Alex's, and I enjoyed being on the sidelines cheering him on as he excelled at this very physical activity. That didn't mean I wasn't planning to take a moment to speak to Maria, but it did mean I'd wait for a break in the action to do so.

"Did you see that goal?" Alex asked as she jumped up and down, clapping and yelling.

"I did," I answered. "I thought for sure it was going to go wide and then it curved back toward the center."

"This is such a close game. I can't help but be nervous for Scooter."

"Yeah, me too. He's been so excited for this tournament. I know he's put in extra practice time with Zak."

"And his hard work paid off. He's doing so awesome."

"He really is." I hugged Alex. "We'll have to have a celebratory dinner after the game." I glanced at the scoreboard and game clock. "It's going to be half time in a few minutes. I need to speak to Tommy's mom. Can you run over and remind Zak to get the orange slices for the kids out of the ice chest?"

Alex looked to where Zak was chatting with one of the other dads. "Yeah, okay. Zak brought bottled water too."

I watched Alex trot away, then turned to locate Maria just as the referee blew the whistle signaling halftime. She'd been chatting with one of the other mothers, but it looked like she was heading to the bathrooms, so I went in that direction.

"Scooter's having the game of his life," Maria commented as I got into line behind her.

"He really is doing well. Tommy too. I can tell he's serious about proving he deserves a spot in the starting lineup. It was fortunate you were able to get tonight off."

"I asked for the night off as soon as I found out about the tournament. The new manager isn't as flexible as the previous one was. It isn't easy to get extra time off beyond what's allotted in your regular schedule."

"It seems like a lot of the old staff has moved on to other jobs since the ownership change."

"Almost half the current employees are new," Maria confirmed. "The new manager is a stickler for procedure and structure. I think the employees who quit felt like they weren't given the appreciation and consideration they deserved. There are times I feel like an employee number who fills a shift rather than a person with needs and desires of my own. If I could find another job that would pay as well, I'd quit in a minute."

I waved at one of the other mothers on Scooter's team and then continued. "I noticed when I was there on Monday that you're in the kitchen now."

"Yes, but not by choice. I'd rather be on the floor, but they said the kitchen was where they needed me. Personally, I find the kitchen boring and I never seem to end up with my share of the tips. I thought about quitting, but like I said before, I need the job. I'm afraid I didn't see you come in on Monday."

"I snuck through the kitchen to use the door out to the alley. You had your back to me."

"Were you there when Ms. Walton's body was found?"

"I'm the one who found her," I confirmed.

"I didn't realize. As soon as we heard what happened, I was asked to help monitor the customers in the dining room. Did you ever find out what happened?"

I shook my head. "Not so far. I did think it was odd that Willa's body was found where it was because it looks as if she was killed elsewhere. Did she spend much time at the restaurant?"

Maria nodded. "She did. Not only did she come by almost every day for lunch but she knew the owner, so she got a discount when she dined with us."

I paused, then said, "I thought the owner lived out of state."

"He lives in Boston, although he travels all the time. I'm not sure how Ms. Walton knew Mr. Bianchi, but I saw them together right after the transfer of ownership. It seemed like they were old friends, not new acquaintances."

Interesting. "Does the owner come to Ashton Falls often?"

"Once a month or so. He likes to check up on things. He never stays more than a few days at a time, but he always joined Ms. Walton for lunch when he was in town. He's here right now. He arrived on Monday and I believe he plans to be in town until Friday morning, although after what happened with Ms. Walton, he may stay longer, seeing how they were friends and all. I'm not sure he can help you figure out what happened, but if you do want to speak to him you should do it before he leaves."

I made a mental note to do just that. I wasn't sure whether Mr. Bianchi was involved in Willa's death, but I couldn't help but wonder how the two knew each other and if their friendship had anything to do with the fact that Willa's body basically had been delivered to Rosie's doorstep.

"I don't suppose you have any idea what Mr. Bianchi and Ms. Walton talked about when they dined together? Did it seem as if they had a business relationship or a personal one?"

Maria shook her head. "I'm not one to listen in on conversations I'm not part of, but you might ask Mr. Bianchi, and if he isn't inclined to share that information with you, I suppose you can talk to Tracy Post." I knew Tracy was one of the waitresses. "She's a nosy sort and has made an art form of lingering if there's an interesting conversation going on. She usually knows everything that's happening with everyone in town."

"I'll do that. Other than Mr. Bianchi, can you think of any employee Willa might have had a friendship with?"

"You're thinking her body was left where it was to serve as some sort of a message or warning to someone who works at the restaurant?"

"That had crossed my mind."

Maria thought about it as the restroom line moved forward. "I know the manager, Ginger Messenger, didn't get along with Ms. Walton at all. They used to glare at each other, and I heard Ginger on the phone with Mr. Bianchi one time complaining that his friend was taking advantage of his generous nature. Of course, based on what I know of him, he isn't generous at all, so I'm not sure what that was all about."

Now that I thought about it, I remembered picking up tension between the two women during the Tuesday morning meetings. I just figured Willa had steamrolled over the new manager the way she had everyone else and that had created an awkward relationship between the two.

"Do you know if Willa came in for lunch on Monday?"

"I didn't see her, but like I said, I was stuck in the kitchen. You might want to speak to some of the other staff."

"I will. And thank you for sharing what you have."

Maria finally made her way to the front of the line, so that was the end of our conversation, but I had a new lead and planned to stop by Rosie's to speak to both Anthony Bianchi and Tracy Post the following day. And it sounded like it might not be a bad idea to speak to Ginger Messenger as long as I was at it.

******

The second half of the game was as awesome as the first and Scooter's team ended up winning by three goals. Scooter wanted pizza for dinner, so the four of us headed over to the local pizza joint.

"Can I play video games while we wait for our food?" Scooter asked.

I glanced at Zak.

"Yeah," Zak answered. "I'll join you. I think you still owe me a rematch of Drone Wars."

Scooter grinned. "Be prepared to be defeated."

I smiled at Zak and Scooter as they headed for the game room. Somehow Scooter had beaten Zak in Drone Wars the last time we were here. I suspected Zak let Scooter win, but he'd never admit that to anyone, not even me.

"So, how was your day?" I asked Alex.

"It was good. I did my oral report for English today."

"And how'd it go?"

Alex shrugged. "It was fine. Phyllis said I got an A, as usual."

"You don't sound very excited," I said. "I know you worked hard on it."

Our eyes met briefly and then Alex glanced down at her hands, which were intertwined on the table.

"Is there something on your mind?" I asked.

Alex raised her head. "I spoke to Phyllis after class. I thought she wanted to speak to me about my report, but she really wanted to talk about the dance. I guess she heard I'd decided not to go and wanted to encourage me to reconsider. I explained about Mark, but she seemed to think I should pull him aside to speak to him. She mentioned that Mark sometimes has difficulty in social situations, so she wasn't surprised he was intimidated by Zak, but she pointed out that he's a nice boy who really seems to like me and was sure we would have fun."

"And what do you think about that?"

"I'm not sure. Everyone I know is going to the dance with a date and I don't want to go alone, but I'm not sure how I feel about asking Mark to reconsider. Zak told me that he would waive the daddy lecture this one time, but I still feel strange about asking someone to go with me who already bailed out on me. Eve says I should look for someone who's worthy of my friendship, not someone like Mark, who's so insecure that he's afraid of a sweetie like Zak. Still, I sort of see Mark's point. Zak's a sweetie, but he can be scary sometimes too. And Phyllis is right that Mark has a hard time in social situations."

I took a moment to consider the situation, then said, "So far you've told me what Phyllis wants you to do and what Eve thinks you should do. What do *you* want to do?"

Alex bit her lip in indecision. She was so brilliant and had such a mature way about her that sometimes I forgot she was still just a kid.

"I like Mark and I guess I can understand why he might have done what he did. I respect Eve. She's a good friend and she's three years older than me. I know she cares about me and doesn't want to see me waste my time with someone who might not be worthy of my time. And I also respect Phyllis, and I know she would never encourage me to do something she felt wasn't good for me."

"You still haven't told me what you want to do."

Alex looked me in the eye. "I want to go to the dance."

"Then I think you should speak to Mark. It's not like you're going to marry the guy; it's just a dance. Zak and I will both be there and if things don't go well one of us can take you home."

Alex nodded slightly. "Okay. I'll call him. If he doesn't already have another date, and if he still wants to go with me, I'll assure him that he can just meet us at the dance as friends and we can casually hang out together."

"That sounds like a wonderful solution. But if you do decide to go to the dance you'll need a dress. We're running out of time, so we'll have to go shopping tomorrow."

******

Later that evening, after the dogs had been walked and the kids tucked into bed, Zak and I curled up on the sofa of the seating area in our suite and enjoyed the cheery fire in the fireplace. Alex had called Mark and they'd worked it out: each would arrive at the dance alone, but they'd meet up and hang out once they got there. Neither were referring to it as a date. That was probably just as well. I could appreciate the difficult situation Alex had found herself in as she tried to navigate a high-school education as a middle-school-aged student.

"I spoke to my mom today," Zak informed me just as I was starting to relax.

"Should I even ask?"

"I know she keeps moving up the date of her visit and I know it's been causing you stress. Initially, she was going to come after the baby was born and then it was Christmas and now she's talking Thanksgiving."

I felt my stomach knot at the very thought of her being here for that long.

"I told her no."

I looked at Zak.

"You told her no?"

"I told her it was important for you and me and Alex and Scooter to prepare for Catherine's arrival as a family. I also told her Pi would be home for a month at Christmas, and because we're doing construction on some of the guest rooms, we really didn't have the extra room for a guest. I could tell she was going to argue, but I didn't give her the chance. I assured her that we'd have a room ready for her by the time the baby was born and we'd of course welcome a short visit at that time but not before."

I reached over and hugged Zak. "Thank you, thank you. I really have been stressing about the whole thing."

"I know. I could tell. And I understand. My mom can be a bit much to take. As I said, she wasn't happy I told her Christmas in Ashton Falls wasn't going to work out, but then I offered to send her and a friend of her choice to Europe for Christmas and she seemed to be excited by the idea."

"That's so sweet of you."

"My mom can be a pain, but she is my mom and I do love her and want her to be happy. She's been talking about Christmas in Europe since I was a child. I think she'll not only enjoy the trip but she'll enjoy planning the trip, which should eliminate her need to be involved in the planning of the nursery."

I kissed Zak hard on the lips. "You're a genius. I owe you big-time."

Zak wrapped his arms around me and pulled me onto his lap. "If you're serious about owing me, I have an idea about how we might work that out."

Chapter 10

Thursday, October 26

Zak had about a half day's work he had to get done, so I called Salinger to ask if he had any news about Willa's death. He didn't have a lot to share other than that he'd confirmed alibis for both Darla Medford and Bruce Rice, so I could officially take them off my suspect list. He'd spoken to Porky too and he, as it turned out, had been with a friend in a bar across town when Willa died.

"Did you check out Tommy Joe's?" I asked.

"I did. The new owner is serving as bartender until they get up and running and he told me he hadn't seen Willa since he'd received his final permit over a month ago. According to him, he didn't have an appointment set up with her and has no idea who TJ might be."

"Do you believe him?"

"Yes. He seemed like a nice guy who didn't have anything to hide."

That left Mortie Sawyer, Matilda Presley, and the still-unidentified TJ. In my mind they were all strong suspects. Salinger had gone to speak to Matilda, who had voluntarily given him a DNA sample. It would take another day to get the results, but in his experience guilty parties usually balked at providing the sample without a warrant, so he suspected the result would come back a negative match to the skin under Willa's fingernails.

I crossed both Darla and Bruce off my list but left both Mortie and Matilda on it for the time being, along with TJ, whoever that turned out to be. Salinger had already looked around Willa's house, but I wanted to look there myself. Zak was busy and I'd promised not to sleuth on my own, so I asked Salinger if he would meet me at the house for a second look and, surprisingly, he agreed.

Willa lived in a tidy home in a nice neighborhood. Her house and yard were immaculately groomed and I suspected she'd had a gardening service come in because I doubted she'd had the time to keep up with the maintenance and she'd lived alone. The front door opened into a foyer, a large square space with three openings. The one to the left led to a large living room with an adjoining kitchen, while the one to the right led to what looked like a combination library and office. On the backside of the foyer was an opening that led to a wide hallway with six doors, four of which were closed. Three of the rooms on the other side of the closed doors seemed to be guest rooms, while the fourth room opened on a laundry room. The first open door was a bathroom and the other, at the end of the hallway, led to a large master suite. From the outside, Willa's house didn't appear as large as it actually was. Given the fact that she lived alone, I wondered why she'd purchased such a large property.

"Everything's neat and tidy," I commented. "It doesn't look as if the house has been broken into and nothing seems to have been disturbed."

"That was the conclusion I came to. The kitchen is clean, the bathrooms are neat and clean, and every bed is made. Either Willa had a maid service or she cleaned over the weekend. The floors are freshly mopped and vacuumed and the windows look to have been recently washed."

"Just because the home is neat doesn't mean it won't provide a clue. Did you look inside the drawers, closets, and cupboards?"

"I peeked in them all. The closets in the guest bedrooms seem to have been used for storage. They contain extra clothing, linens, and boxes. The dresser drawers in the guest bedrooms are empty. The guest bathroom, likewise, doesn't have any personal items. The kitchen is stocked with all the usual items you'd find in a kitchen. I didn't find anything odd. Willa's bedroom suite, of course, had the most personal items, followed by her home office. I'm not sure what we can hope to find if we don't know what we're looking for. Nothing jumped out to me as being obviously out of place when I looked through on Tuesday."

"Do you mind if I just look around a bit?"

Salinger handed me a pair of gloves. "Knock yourself out, but don't remove anything from the premises. I have some calls to return, so I'm going to have a seat at the kitchen table while you explore. Holler if you see something."

On the surface, it didn't seem as if there would be anything to find, but my gut told me if something was going on in Willa's life there would be a clue to be found in her private space. It did seem as if the bedroom and office would be my best bets; I decided to start with the office.

The room was lovely, with a cream-colored carpet, an antique white desk, and an entire wall full of bookshelves. There was a small fireplace framed with white brick and a light blue sofa under one window. I sat down at the desk and began opening drawers. There were quite a few file folders all neatly labeled and filed alphabetically in the two bottom drawers. Other drawers held scissors, glue, tape, sticky notes, and other items you'd expect to find in an office. The drawer at the top left of the desk was locked. I looked around but didn't see a key. If there was anything worth finding it would probably be in that drawer.

I got up to take a quick look at the bookshelves. One photo in particular caught my eye, of four children, all around the age of ten, standing in front of a big pond. All the children—one boy and three girls—wore shorts and T-shirts and all had muddy feet, as if they'd been wading in the water.

I picked up the photo to take a closer look. There were mud smudges on their faces and they were smiling at the photographer. Based on the green grass and the lush landscape it seemed the photo must have been taken in the early summer. I couldn't tell where it had been taken, but it occurred to me to check the back, so I carefully removed it from the frame and turned it over. On the back was written *Moss Lake* and then the names *Wanda, TJ, Ginny, and Willa.*

The TJ on Willa's calendar must have been someone she knew from childhood. The entry on the calendar only had the initials and not the purpose for the calendar entry, so I'd supposed it was equally likely she was meeting this person as that she'd made a note to call him—and it seemed from the list of names it was a him. Now I supposed the entry could even have been a reminder to take some action, such as sending a birthday card or returning a message. I wondered if Salinger had found Wanda because it occurred to me Willa's sister would have at least one of the answers we were after.

"I found something," I said as I walked into the dining area and sat down across from him. I handed the photo to Salinger and waited a moment for him to look at it.

"What am I looking at?"

"Read the back."

Understanding dawned on his face after he turned it over.

"Did you ever get a hold of Wanda?"

"I was able to contact a prior boss of hers. He hadn't spoken to her for a couple of years, but he did say he'd heard she passed away."

I frowned. "I'm sorry to hear that. Do you know when it happened?"

"Just a few weeks ago. I did some additional investigation and found out she was killed in a car accident."

"And you didn't think that was worth mentioning to me?"

Salinger shrugged. "I just found out yesterday. I guess it hadn't come up. I was going to tell you."

"Wanda died three weeks before her sister was murdered. Don't you think they could be linked in some way?"

"It occurred to me, but I had a long chat with the officer who responded to the accident. Wanda was alone in the car and there were a dozen eyewitnesses who saw her drive into the side of a building after she swerved to avoid hitting a dog. I don't see how a random accident and a murder can be related."

I looked at the photo again. "The way it happened, it does sound like an accident, but I don't believe in coincidences. I think we need to find out who this TJ is. Willa and Wanda grew up in Boston, and it looks like they were friends with this TJ since they were children. There must be someone who knows who the boy is. Willa has mentioned that both her parents are dead and Wanda might have been her only sibling, but maybe we can find an aunt, uncle, or cousin."

"I'll see what I can do. Did you find anything else?"

"There's a locked drawer in the desk. Do you have a key?"

"No."

"Do you think we should try to open it?"

"I don't have permission from the owner of the home to break in, nor do I have probable cause to do so."

Okay, I knew the drill. "I want to look in the bedroom, so I'll be a few more minutes."

"You have ten and then we need to get going."

I figured I could come back later and snoop around in the bedroom if I felt I needed to, but right now I wanted to see what was in the desk. I headed into the bathroom to look for a nail file or something equally likely to be useful in picking the small lock. I found a multipurpose tool that included a nail file, scissors, and nail clippers and figured it would have to do. I returned to the desk and began to work on the lock. It took me a few minutes, but eventually I managed to get it open. Inside was a file folder with handwritten notes, newspaper articles, and official-looking reports. A quick glance indicated the contents covered several different events, including Wanda's car accident. I knew Salinger wouldn't let me take the file and I didn't have time to explore the contents right then, so I went into the bedroom and grabbed a sweater from Willa's closet. I put it on over my T-shirt to add bulk, then slipped the file under my shirt. Hopefully, Salinger wouldn't notice I hadn't worn a sweater into the house.

******

"I don't know what this all means," I said to Ellie later that morning in answer to her question about the file I'd managed to get away with. "The folder contains information regarding three incidents: the death of Willa's sister in an automobile accident three weeks ago; the death of someone named Tamara Stewart, who lived in San Francisco, as the result of an allergic reaction to nuts eight weeks ago, and the death of Gwen Farmer, who died five weeks ago in a house fire in Portland, Oregon."

"Maybe Willa knew the other two women or maybe she noticed some sort of a link in the three deaths." Ellie suggested. "It'll be hard to know unless she referred to her interest in the deaths in her notes. Have you read them?"

"I've browsed them. The notes seem to pertain to the cases themselves, but so far, I haven't found any mention of why she was interested in the other two deaths. Salinger hurried me out of the house, but I feel like we need to go back there to look around some more."

"*We*?"

I glanced at Eli, who was sitting happily in his swing. "Maybe not *we*. Maybe Zak and me. Later. After he finishes his work for the day." I furrowed my brow as I tried to sort things in my mind. Did Willa know something that got her killed? And what about TJ? Was he in some way related to everything that was going on?

"How about lunch?" I asked. "My treat."

"Why?" Ellie asked, suspicion clearly evident in her voice.

"I want to speak to one of the waitstaff at Rosie's. We'll be in a restaurant full of a lunchtime crowd, so neither of us will be in any danger."

"What about Eli?"

"You can bring him or I can call my mom to ask her to watch him."

In the end, we decided to leave Eli with my mother. While simply talking to a couple of staff members was a pretty danger-free activity, Ellie didn't want Eli around anything that could in any way be considered sleuthing, and I guess I didn't blame her.

When we arrived at Rosie's we asked for a table in Tracy's section. It was a weekday in the off season, so even though it was close to lunchtime, the place wasn't crowded. Ellie and I ordered drinks, which gave me a few minutes to figure out how to broach the subject of conversations Tracy may have overheard, at least in terms of those connected to Willa. After a bit of thought I decided the direct approach was probably best.

"I guess you heard about Willa Walton," I said when she set our drinks in front of us.

"It's all over town."

"I know Willa came in here for lunch almost every day. Did she say anything or did you overhear anything that might have led you to believe she was in some sort of trouble?"

"Willa dined by herself a lot of the time, which meant she usually read, so there wasn't much conversation going on."

"Do you remember the last person she had lunch with?"

"Mr. Bianchi on Monday. He'd just flown in from San Francisco and Willa and he shared a meal most times he was in town. They seemed like they knew each other from before he bought the place."

"Do you know where Mr. Bianchi is staying? I'd like to ask him about his lunch with Willa."

"I think he usually stays at the inn on Fourth Street. I guess if you want to know for certain you can ask Ginger. I'm sure she has all the details."

"Do you happen to know what Willa and Mr. Bianchi talked about on Monday?"

Tracy tapped her pen against her order pad. "They were speaking real quiet and they sat in the booth all the way in the back, but it seemed like they might have been talking about her sister."

I guess that made sense. If Mr. Bianchi was an old friend he may very well have known Wanda as well as Willa.

"Is there anyone else Willa dined with over the course of the past two weeks?"

"She had lunch with Hazel last week, and there was another lady I didn't recognize a couple of weeks ago. I think she was from out of town."

"Did you catch her name?"

Tracy shook her head. "Willa paid and she never introduced us. Can I get you some food? We have club sandwiches on special today."

Ellie and I both ordered and Tracy headed toward the kitchen.

"So, what are you thinking?" Ellie asked.

"If Willa had lunch with Hazel she might have told her about Wanda. Do you mind if we stop off at the library after this?"

"No, I don't mind."

"I also want to speak to Mr. Bianchi. If he knew Willa before he bought Rosie's he might know something about her past that would help us understand what happened. Willa and I weren't close, but I can't believe her sister died and she never mentioned it."

"I guess that might be why she was distracted at the committee meeting last week and why she thought she might miss this week. Maybe she was working on plans to head back East."

"I suppose." My instinct told me everything we knew so far had to be in some way related, but I was struggling to come up with how.

"You know, I just thought of something else," Tracy said as she set our meals in front of us. "I don't know if it's important, but it could be."

"What's that?" I asked as I cut my sandwich in quarters.

"Mr. Bianchi planned to visit his restaurant in Denver when he left Ashton Falls, but Willa was insisting he go to Portland to look in to something there. I'm not sure why she wanted him to go to Portland, but she seemed adamant. Mr. Bianchi tried to explain that he had a schedule he liked to stick to, but Willa didn't want to take no for an answer. When they saw I was nearby they stopped talking, but I could see the discussion was important to both of them."

"Thank you, Tracy. That may end up being important."

Ellie frowned at me but didn't say anything. Once Tracy was out of earshot I leaned forward and whispered to Ellie,

"One of the deaths Willa had notes on happened in Portland."

Chapter 11

The library was within walking distance from Rosie's, so Ellie and I headed there first. It was a lovely day for a walk, with the crisp cool air and fall leaves in full color. Ellie and I hadn't spent nearly as much time together since she'd had Eli as we once had, so it was nice to spend a few hours together, even if we were investigating the death of a friend.

"I'm excited to take Eli to the Hamlet this year," Ellie commented as we walked along the leaf-covered sidewalk. "I know he's too young to really understand what's going on, but I think he'll like the colorful lights and the bells and whistles that come from the games."

"I imagine there's a certain magic in firsts. Next Halloween will be Catherine's first and I'm excited for that already. Are you going to carve a pumpkin with him?"

"I'm going to try, although he'll probably want to eat the innards, so he may have to watch from his high chair. I got a mechanical Frankenstein for the entry and he thinks it's the funniest thing ever when it moves its arms and talks."

"He's not scared of it?"

"Not at all. He's a pretty even-tempered baby. He seems to be happy all the time and he laughs more than any six-month-old I've ever met. I can't wait to try his Cookie Monster costume on him."

"I figured you'd have done that the day you bought it."

"I would have. If things had been different."

I took Ellie's hand in mine and gave it a squeeze as we climbed the steps to the front door of the library. There was a huge maple tree at the entrance, so red and orange leaves covered the entire patio area. It really was a beautiful time of year.

"Zoe; Ellie," Hazel greeted us. "How nice of you to stop by."

"We wanted to see how you were doing and to ask about your lunch with Willa last week."

"I'm hanging in there. It's been hard, and I keep wondering what I could have done that might have helped her. She didn't have a lot of people she was close to. I imagine I was closer to her than most. I should have made more of an effort."

"You couldn't have known what would happen," Ellie said.

"True, but as I said at the committee meeting, I could tell something was wrong. I should have dug harder when she seemed not to want to talk about it. Do you know if Sheriff Salinger has been in touch with her sister? I'd like to call her to pay my respects."

I glanced at Ellie, whose eyes had gotten as large as silver dollars.

"Wanda is dead," I said, before taking the time to come up with a better way of approaching such a sensitive subject.

"Dead? Whatever do you mean?"

"She died in an auto accident three weeks ago. I assumed you knew. In fact, I was going to ask you about it."

Hazel sat down on the chair behind her. Her face had gone pale and she looked momentarily dazed. "I can't believe Willa didn't say anything." She looked at me with a tear in the corner of her eye. "We had lunch last week and she never said a word."

"I thought it was odd that no one seemed to know about it, but I'm very surprised she didn't confide in you."

Hazel dipped her head. "I guess we weren't as close as I believed."

I sat down next to Hazel and took her hand in mine. "I don't think it was that. I think something was, and probably still is, going on. Willa had a file in the desk of her home office with information pertaining to three deaths that occurred in the past eight weeks. On the surface, I don't see how a death in San Francisco and another in Portland could be related to each other and Willa's death in Ashton Falls and Wanda's death in Boston, but newspaper articles about the deaths, along with corresponding notes in Willa's handwriting, were in the same file, so maybe…"

"So you think Willa's death was related to those other three?" Hazel asked.

"I don't know," I admitted. "I think at this point we have to have an open mind and look at any and all clues that might present themselves. I have to consider that the file and its contents are clues."

"Did you find anything else?" Hazel asked.

I nodded. "Yes. On the bookshelf in Willa's office was a photo of four children. On the back, someone had written *Moss*

Lake and four names: *Wanda, Willa, Ginny*, and *TJ*. Did Willa ever mention a TJ to you?"

Hazel shook her head. "No, not that I can remember. Willa never talked about her past or her life outside of Ashton Falls much. I'm not sure if something bad happened, but she seemed to want to distance herself from her life before she moved here. She never went away on holidays, and although she mentioned Wanda a time or two in passing, she never really talked about her." Hazel bowed her head for a moment before looking back up. "How can I help?"

I didn't reply right away. I knew Hazel needed to be involved for her own piece of mind, but I wasn't sure Zak would consider her an adequate babysitter for his pregnant wife, so I didn't think she could help with the actual sleuthing.

"The file you found: maybe I can do some research on the deaths in the file," Hazel suggested. "I have time and resources here at work to do something like that. If I run into a stumbling block we can always bring Zak in on it."

Zak was busy and Hazel did have time. Maybe it was a good idea to let her do some of the ground work. "Okay. We'll make a copy of everything in the file. I'll keep one set and give you the other. We should keep this between ourselves and the usual sleuthing gang. We know someone killed Willa here in Ashton Falls. Whatever we do, we don't want that someone to find out we know about the file or the other deaths. I don't know for certain they had anything to do with Willa's death, but I have a strong suspicion it will turn out they do."

"I assume it's okay to speak to your grandpa about it. He's coming for dinner tonight and I hoped we could discuss the options."

"You can talk to Grandpa. Zak and Levi obviously know, as do my parents. I'm sure the subject of Willa's death will come up at book club tonight. I'm comfortable discussing the specifics with Phyllis and Ethan, but not the rest. If we want to get their input we'll ask them to stay after."

"Agreed. I'll let you set the pace."

I hugged Hazel. "Thank you. We'll find out who killed Willa and make them pay."

Hazel copied the files, then Ellie and I headed over to the inn where Tracy thought Mr. Bianchi might be staying. The clerk at the desk informed us that he had stayed there in the past but wasn't currently checked in, nor did she expect him. I thanked her and Ellie and I headed to my parents' house to pick up Eli.

My parents were sitting at the dining table discussing Willa's death when we arrived.

"How'd it go?" my mom asked.

"Tracy didn't seem to know a lot, and we spoke to Hazel, who had no idea Willa's sister had died. She was pretty upset about it and wanted to help, so I agreed to let her research the news articles I found in Willa's desk. I don't know for certain they're related to Willa's death, but they might be."

"Do you have any strong suspects from the local pool?" Dad asked.

"I have two left: Mortie Sawyer, who owned the blanket Willa was wrapped in, and Matilda Presley, who had scratches on her face. Both had pretty huge beefs with Willa. I think either could have done it. Salinger got Matilda to agree to a DNA sample, so we just need to wait for the results. Other than that, I don't have any strong suspects. I'm interested in the new owner of Rosie's. According to his staff, he was in town on Monday and had lunch with Willa. He lives in Boston, which is where Wanda lived, and he'd just come from San Francisco, which is where the first victim, Tamara Stewart, who died eight weeks ago of an allergic reaction to nuts, lived. One of the waitresses told us Willa was trying to get Bianchi to go to Portland next instead of Denver, which is where he was supposed to go. The third victim, Gwen Farmer, died in a house fire in Portland five weeks ago."

"Are you suggesting this man is responsible for all four deaths?" Dad asked.

"Not necessarily, but he might be linked to the victims in some way. Anthony Bianchi owns businesses across the country. Maybe all the victims were connected to the businesses he owns." I ran a hand through my hair in frustration. "I don't know if he's involved, but he seems to be a good enough suspect to follow up on."

"Just let us know how we can help, sweetheart," Dad said.

"Right now, Zak and I, Ellie and Levi, you and Mom, and Hazel, know what's going on. I told Hazel she could tell Grandpa, who'll be at her house for dinner before book club, and we may bring Ethan and Phyllis into it if there's an opportunity to speak to them privately. Both have exceptional minds and Ethan seems to have a knack for investigation. Don't mention the investigation to anyone else.

Willa was killed in Ashton Falls and the killer may very well still be in the area. I don't want to put any of us in danger."

"Of course, dear. We won't mention it to a soul," Mom assured me.

I drove Ellie home, then went to the house to see how Zak was doing. I could see he was harassed and frustrated, so I promised him I was done sleuthing for the day and he could continue to work. My plan was to pick up the kids from school, drop Scooter at the house, and then take Alex dress-shopping. I'd pick up some takeout for dinner and then go to book club. Zak looked relieved that he'd have the rest of the day to do his work. The next few days were going to be busy for the Zimmerman clan and I wanted to make them as easy for him as possible.

******

"I like the design of the purple dress, but the color is a bit much," Alex said later that afternoon. We were in the third and last dress shop in town and hadn't found anything quite right. "I want something simple. Pretty but not overly sexy, if you know what I mean."

"I do and I agree."

"And I'm not a fan of bright colors. What about black? It *is* a Halloween dance."

I looked around the store, but nothing stood out.

"Maybe we should have brought Grandma," Alex murmured. She had started calling my mother Grandma a while back and, surprisingly, my young and sophisticated mother hadn't minded a bit.

"That's a great idea. I'll call her to see if she can meet us."

Luckily for both Alex and me, my mom was home and delighted to help. As soon as Mom arrived, she grabbed an armful of dresses and ushered Alex back into the dressing room. I didn't figure I had much to add, so I wandered around the store looking at dresses that would never fit. At least not until after Catherine was born.

"Zoe Donovan, is that you?"

I turned around and smiled at the tall blond woman behind me. "Veronica. How are you? It's been ages."

Veronica hugged me and I hugged her back.

"I'm in town for a family reunion," she explained. "I heard about Willa. I can't believe someone would do such a thing to such a lovely woman."

Veronica had interned in Willa's office when she was a senior in high school and the two had gotten along fabulously.

"Have you heard what happened?" Veronica asked.

"I don't think the sheriff knows yet."

"I'm sure he must have suspects."

"I'm sure he does, but there's a lot of information to go through. Had you stayed in touch with Willa after you graduated and went off to college?"

"We sent Christmas cards every year, but not really. You know how it is; first there was college and then I was trying to build a career. Once my career took off I got married and had a child. Life tends to fly by when you aren't paying attention."

"It really does," I agreed.

"I heard you married Zak Zimmerman."

I nodded.

"Any kids?"

I put my hand on my stomach. "Almost."

Veronica smiled. "You're expecting? How wonderful. Boy or girl?"

"Girl. Catherine. She's due in January."

Veronica hugged me again. "Well, congratulations."

"Thank you. Listen, Roni, I know you and Willa were close for a while. The sheriff is trying to track down Willa's next of kin. Her sister, Wanda, passed away."

"Wanda's dead? When did that happen?"

"Just three weeks ago. Car accident."

Veronica looked genuinely distressed. "I'm so sorry to hear that. She was a nice woman."

"Do you know who else he might want to contact?"

"Stephi, of course."

"Stephi?"

"Stephi is Wanda's daughter. I met her a couple of times when I was in college."

"That's right. I forgot you went to Harvard."

"Willa arranged for me to have Thanksgiving with Wanda and Stephi my first year of college. I couldn't afford to come home and they were nearby."

"Do you have contact information for Stephi?"

Veronica nodded. "I have an address book on my computer. I can text you the information when I get back to my parents'. I know Wanda and Stephi had a falling out over a man a few years ago. I'm not sure they ever reconciled."

"Stephi was dating a man Wanda didn't approve of?"

"Actually, Wanda was dating a man Stephi didn't approve of."

Chapter 12

"It's black with little fringy things along the bottom." Alex was describing the dress we'd purchased and my mom had taken home to slightly alter as we enjoyed a family meal that evening.

"It sounds nice," Zak answered. "I can't wait to see it."

"Grandma's going to come over tomorrow to help me dress and do my hair. I think we're going to curl it. I wasn't sure I even wanted to go to the dance, but now I can't wait."

I smiled at Zak, who winked at me.

"Am I going home from school with Tucker tomorrow?" Scooter asked. Because Alex, Zak, and I were all spending the evening at the dance we'd arranged for Scooter to spend the night with his best friend.

"Yes," I answered. "Tucker's aunt will pick you both up from school. Haunted Hamlet begins on Saturday, so we'll pick both you and Tucker up at around nine. I'm supposed to be at the kiddie carnival at ten."

"I don't want to play the kiddie games. I want to go to the corn maze and the haunted house," Scooter countered.

"Zak can take you while I do my shift." I pushed my plate aside. "I need to run up to get ready for book club. I bought some cookies from the bakery while Alex and I were in town if any of you want dessert."

I left my family to their discussion of the best Hamlet events while Charlie and I headed upstairs to get changed. Maybe I'd bring him with me tonight. Hazel wouldn't mind. In fact, I used to bring him all the time, though lately I'd taken to leaving him behind. I missed having him by my side everywhere I went, and I suspected Charlie missed it as well.

I was trying to decide between a pullover sweater that would definitely show off my baby bump and a cardigan over a blouse when my phone rang. Based on the caller ID, I assumed it was Wanda's daughter, Stephi, calling me back.

"Hello," I said.

"This is Stephi Grant. I'm returning your call regarding my aunt."

I sat down on the corner of my bed. "Yes; thank you for calling me back. My name is Zoe Zimmerman. I live in Ashton Falls. I ran into Veronica Newton, who gave me your number. I wanted to be sure you'd been notified that your Aunt Willa passed away this week."

"Yes, I heard. A friend of my mother called to tell me what happened."

"I'm working with the sheriff to try to figure out how your aunt died. Had you spoken to her recently?"

"No. My mom and Aunt Willa didn't get along all that well. She rarely visited us in Boston and I never visited her in Ashton Falls. I only met Veronica because Aunt Willa arranged an introduction when Roni lived in the area. We weren't superclose, but I guess you could say we were friends, although I haven't seen or talked to her in years."

"I understand your mother died recently as well."

There was a pause before Stephi answered. "Yes. She died in a car accident three weeks ago."

"I'm very sorry for your loss. I'm sure it must be very difficult to have both your mother and your aunt pass within a few weeks of each other."

"I wasn't really close to either of them. Is there something specific I can help you with?"

I could tell by the catch in her voice that Stephi wasn't as unaffected as she tried to sound. Still, I wasn't sure what she could tell me that I didn't already know. Unless... "Do you know someone named TJ?"

"Unfortunately. Why do you want to know about that loser?"

"Your Aunt Willa had an appointment with someone named TJ on the day she died. I've been trying to track down who that might be."

"TJ's name is Tony. He grew up with my mom and Aunt Willa. I guess they were all close friends, along with someone named Ginny."

"Do you have contact information for Ginny?"

"No. I know she developed some psychological issues during her late teens. My mom mentioned she was institutionalized when she was in her early twenties. I'm not sure what happened after that. It didn't seem like Mom kept in touch with her."

"And TJ?"

"My mom was living with the moron right up until the day she died. I have no idea what she saw in him; he's a total ass. I tried to talk her into breaking things off with him, but she wouldn't hear of it. It destroyed our relationship."

"So TJ lives in Boston?"

"Yeah, he lives in Boston. Like I said, he was shacking up with my mom or, more accurately, she was shacking up with him because he lived in this ostentatious mansion and invited her to move in with him. Why is this important again?"

"Could your mother's boyfriend have been in Ashton Falls this week?"

"Yeah, he could have been there. He owns a bunch of businesses and travels all the time. I heard he bought something near where Willa lived."

Suddenly a light went on. "Is TJ a nickname for Anthony Bianchi Jr.?"

"Yes, although he never goes by Anthony. It's either TJ or Tony. TJ hated the fact that he had his dad's name. He always said he wanted to be his own man. Too bad he didn't try harder to be a decent man instead of the snake he ended up being."

"Is there a specific reason you didn't get along with TJ?"

"He cheated on my mother every chance he got. And he didn't even try to hide the fact he had a woman in every town. My mom said she didn't care and was happy for the time they shared. The whole arrangement made me so angry. My mom was an intelligent, hardworking person who gave up her career to be kept by a man who didn't deserve her. I couldn't stand seeing them together, so I distanced myself. As far as I'm concerned, the snake cheated me out of the last years of my mother's life."

I hated to even ask this, but I knew I had to. "Do you think Willa could have been one of TJ's women?"

"Sure, if she was fooled by him the way my mother was. The guy seemed to have this power over women that left them brainless fools. I could never understand it."

I spoke to Stephi a while longer, then called Salinger to fill him in on the newest development in what was becoming a completely absurd murder case. No matter how hard I tried, I couldn't picture Willa being a kept woman to some modern-day Casanova, but it certainly would explain a lot.

****

By the time I reached Hazel's for book club the rest of the gang had already arrived. I could see I wasn't going to have a chance to pull Hazel, Grandpa, Phyllis, and Ethan aside until the discussion was concluded, so I settled in to Hazel's cozy living room to participate to the best of my ability about a book I hadn't read. To be honest, I rarely got around to reading the books, but the others understood that about me and no one seemed to care.

As she did every year, Hazel had decorated for the season in an elegant, classy way. The fire that crackled merrily in the fireplace provided a nice backdrop to the scented candles, seasonal floral displays, and antique decorations. The book we were discussing was a thriller that, based on the discussion, was probably one I would enjoy, if life ever slowed down enough to allow me to read a book.

I pulled Phyllis and Ethan aside during the break and asked if they could stay after the meeting broke up. It appeared they'd come together and both agreed they could. While I didn't know it for certain, it appeared as if Ethan and Phyllis's relationship may have taken a romantic turn. Both were in their sixties, both had worked their entire lives in academia, and neither had ever married. It didn't seem either were in the market for romance, but if they were, I couldn't think of a better pairing.

I managed to listen to the discussion for almost an hour before my mind wandered. The idea that Willa was involved romantically with the man her sister was living with didn't sit well with me. Stephi clearly didn't care for him, and I had no doubt her feelings toward him were based in some level of reality, but sisters? Even if he was up for it I couldn't see how Willa would be. A better explanation was that they'd renewed their childhood friendship when he bought Rosie's and began spending time in Ashton Falls. Of course, if that was all that had been going on, I couldn't see how that had gotten Willa killed.

I thought about the other women in Willa's file. I hadn't had the opportunity to study the information in depth, but there'd been photos, and both Gwen and Tamara were attractive women who looked to be in their mid- to late-forties. I'd need to dig deeper to see if I could find a connection between TJ and them. Could they have also been involved with him in a romantic way? If that was the case, had he killed all four women? Or could there be a fifth woman taking care of the competition?

I glanced at Hazel, who was looking at me in an odd way. I narrowed my gaze and hoped I hadn't been mumbling out loud. I did that sometimes when my mind was really focused on something I was trying to work out. I glanced at Charlie, who was sitting at my feet. He was watching the group and didn't seem to be paying attention to me, which meant I was probably safe. If I'd been mumbling it would have attracted his attention.

Once the discussion wrapped up and everyone other than Hazel, Grandpa, Phyllis, and Ethan left, we gathered around the dining table and I filled them in on what I'd learned to date. "Did you manage to look at the file I left with you?' I asked Hazel when I'd finished my spiel.

"Yes, I did," Hazel confirmed. "The first victim, Tamara Stewart, lived in San Francisco. She died eight weeks ago of an allergic reaction. She was severely allergic to peanuts, and friends reported she kept an EpiPen with her at all times. On the night she died she bought takeout from a restaurant in which she frequently dined. She ordered a carton of the same sausage soup she'd eaten dozens of times and a loaf of bread. She took her meal down to the beach, where she planned to sit in her car to watch the sunset. She was alone in the car when it appeared she must have had an immediate and severe allergic reaction to the soup. She certainly didn't have time to get help or call anyone. Her EpiPen wasn't found at the scene, so it was assumed neither the one she carried in her purse nor the one she kept in her glove compartment were available to her. A passerby eventually noticed she was in trouble and stopped to help, but she died before she got to the hospital."

"Sounds suspicious," I said.

"Very," Hazel agreed.

"Were there notes in the file relating to who might have had access to the soup, who knew she planned to buy it, and who might have had access to her car and her purse and might have removed the EpiPens?"

"Initially, the death was ruled an accident. It was assumed a safety protocol of some sort had been violated in the restaurant kitchen resulting in peanut oil making its way into the soup. Willa must have believed otherwise and began digging into it. I don't know that she came to any conclusions, but she seemed to be working on the assumption that the peanut oil was deliberately added to the soup and the death staged to look like an accident."

Hazel paused to give everyone a chance to respond before moving on to the second death in the file.

"The next woman was Gwen Farmer. She lived in Portland, Oregon, and died in a house fire. She was asleep in her bed when the fire started. She either was overcome by smoke before she even woke up or she was passed out after a night of partying. Either way, it appeared she never attempted to escape the flames."

"She must really have been out of it not to realize her house was on fire," Grandpa offered.

"What if it wasn't an accident?" I asked. "What if she was given drugs to make her pass out or if she was already dead when the fire started? The fact that Willa, who's now dead, was looking in to it leads me to believe she at least believed something fishy was going on."

Hazel set the file aside and adjusted her glasses. "It occurred to me that the fire seemed staged as well. I can't imagine not waking up when the house around you is on fire. There wasn't a mention in the article Willa had or the notes she made that the police suspected foul play, but I'd be surprised if there wasn't an investigation. Perhaps Salinger can get additional information."

"I'll talk to him about it," I assured Hazel.

"How does Wanda's death figure into all this?" Phyllis asked.

"Wanda died in a car accident three weeks ago in Boston. Witnesses stated that she swerved to avoid hitting a dog, overcorrected, and hit a wall, resulting in a fatal head injury. Willa had made notes relating to the mechanical condition of the car. I think she was looking for tampering, but she never said whether she found it or not. On the surface, it appeared to be a genuine accident, but I found something moderately interesting that seemed to be more so only after hearing about Zoe's conversation with Wanda's daughter, Stephi. It turns out the wall Wanda hit after she swerved was the west wall of a building owned by her boyfriend, Anthony Bianchi."

"So Wanda died after hitting the wall of a building owned by this TJ and three weeks later Willa's body was dumped at the back door of a building he owned all the way across the country. That can't be a coincidence," I said.

"It wouldn't seem so," Hazel agreed.

"What about the woman who died from the peanut oil in the soup?" Ethan asked. "Were her actions on the night of her death in any way related to Mr. Bianchi?"

"I'm not sure," Hazel said. "If they were it didn't say as much in the notes."

"The guy owns a bunch of restaurants," Grandpa pointed out. "Maybe he owned the restaurant where the soup was bought."

"I'll see if I can find out," Hazel offered.

"If the information isn't readily available call Zak," I instructed. "I'm sure he can dig up the ownership information for the restaurant."

Hazel made a few notes and set the file aside.

"I think we should assume there may be more going on than meets the eye in all these cases," Grandpa said.

"What's the plan from this point?" Phyllis asked.

No one answered right away. Based on the focused look of the group everyone was trying to make sense of the seemingly unrelated pieces of information we'd gathered.

"Why don't we look for a link between all the victims?" Ethan suggested. "We can see if and how they're related to one another and if and how they're related to

Anthony Bianchi. My guess is either he's behind all the deaths and we'll need to prove he's the killer or someone related to him, such as one of his lovers, is behind the deaths."

"I agree," I said. "Looking for the connection seems as good a place to move forward as any."

"I'm not all that busy, while Hazel has the library to run, so why don't I take a stab at it?" Ethan offered. "Maybe we should all gather again tomorrow."

"We have the dance at Zimmerman Academy," I said. "But we should be home by ten, if you all want to come over to the house then."

Everyone agreed that would be acceptable. Ten was late for me these days, but I really wanted to get Willa's murder solved and I wanted to do it without putting Catherine into any danger. Sleuthing as part of a group seemed the way to go.

Chapter 13

Friday, October 27

I woke the next morning to the sound of hammering. I slowly opened my eyes and looked around. Both Zak and Charlie were gone and the clock on the bedside table informed me that it was nine o'clock. I rarely slept that late, but I hadn't been sleeping all that well lately, so maybe my body needed to get caught up.

I rolled out of bed and slipped a knee-length sweatshirt over my head. The blackout blinds had been drawn, so I pulled them aside and looked out over the yard. The hammering I'd heard had been Zak putting up even more lights. It was a good thing my Halloween husband was rich because I had a feeling our electric bill was going to rival the national debt.

Based on the time, I assumed the kids were already at school. I could see all three dogs were watching Zak, so I snuck downstairs for a cup of herbal tea. The first thing I noticed there was the wonderful smell of the cinnamon roll Zak had left warming in the oven. I poured a dollop of cream into my tea and sat down at the table to organize my day.

I had a call from Hillary's mother, letting me know her husband had agreed to adopt the orange and white kitten and hoped to pick it up today. I could let Jeremy handle the adoption, but I wanted to see to this one personally, so I agreed to meet the mother and daughter at the Zoo at one-thirty, after the elementary school let out for the day.

I also wanted to go by to speak to Matilda Presley's neighbor. I wasn't sure if the barking dog and the fight that had been caused by it was just a convenient excuse to explain the scratches on Matilda's face, but if there was any chance—even a small one—that Matilda really might poison it, it was better I tried to come up with a solution.

My mom was coming over at four o'clock to help Alex get ready for the dance, so I needed to complete all my errands by that time. I glanced at the stack of boxes in the drive and realized Zak was going to be occupied the rest of the day. If he was taking time off work to decorate he must have completed the software project he'd been working on the past couple of weeks. He worked hard, but I knew how much Halloween meant to him, so I decided to take a day off from sleuthing so he could relax and have some fun.

I finished my cinnamon roll and went upstairs to shower and dress. It looked as if it was going to be a perfect autumn day, so I dressed in a pair of black leggings and a burnt orange sweater that was full enough to minimize my bump. I'd need to deal with the clothing issue eventually, but today wasn't going to be that day. I pulled my hair up into a sloppy bun and headed for the back patio, where Zak was currently doing something with a fog machine.

"I hope the weather holds for our party on Tuesday," I said after giving Zak a quick kiss on the cheek. "You've really outdone yourself in the decorations department this year."

"I checked the forecast and there isn't a drop of rain predicted until well into November. I thought we could create a spooky setting out here with the fog and the lights. I have a sound machine hooked up as well."

"It sounds awesome. I think Scooter and his friends will enjoy the authenticity."

"I invited a bunch of the kids from the Academy as well. I know they're a little older then the kids we usually invite, but I figure you're never too old for a good scare."

My six-and-a-half-foot-tall husband looked like a kid himself when he was working on his creations. "I can see you're busy, so I'll leave you to your work. I have a few errands to run, but I should be back well before my mom gets here to help Alex get dressed."

Zak stopped what he was doing and looked me in the eye. "You aren't going out sleuthing?"

"No sleuthing. I promise. I may go by to speak to Salinger, but that's it. I'm going over to the Zoo to spend a few hours there and then I'm going to see if Ellie wants to meet for lunch. After that I have an adoption and then I'll be home."

I could tell by the look on Zak's face that he wasn't 100 percent sure I was telling him everything, but I guess he decided to trust me because he kissed me once, then made me promise to call him if my plans changed. Charlie was sitting at my feet looking up at me with expectation on his face, so I decided to take him with me.

Once I got to the Zoo, I caught up with Jeremy, then called Ellie and arranged to meet her for lunch. I still had an hour and a half until I needed to meet her and Eli, so I thought I'd use the time to check in with Salinger. I hoped he'd have new information that would allow us to focus a bit. The longer it took to find Willa's killer, the less likely we would be to do so.

"Please tell me you have news," I jumped right in.

"I have news. The DNA under Willa's fingernails doesn't match Matilda Presley. Although she has a somewhat toxic personality, I don't think she's our killer."

Things would have been easier if she'd done it, but eliminating her as a suspect did move us closer to the truth. "I guess that leaves Mortie Sawyer, Anthony Bianchi, and someone related to Anthony Bianchi," I summarized.

"Wait...How did Anthony Bianchi get on the list?"

"I have some stuff to tell you, but if you don't want to have to lock up your pregnant sidekick you might not want to ask me where I got the information."

Salinger groaned and agreed. I filled him in on the file I'd discovered and how we'd come to believe it may have been related to Willa's death.

"Okay, let me get this straight," Salinger began. "Somehow you magically got your hands on a file with information on three deaths in it, and now you think they're all related to Willa's?"

"Correct."

"And you've learned the TJ Willa noted on her calendar and appeared to have been planning to meet with on the day she died is the new owner of Rosie's, Anthony Bianchi."

"Correct. Although he doesn't like to be called Anthony, which was also his father's name, and goes by Tony or TJ."

Salinger cleared his throat before continuing. "And you're saying this TJ had not only been shacking up with Willa's sister prior to her death but was a childhood friend of both of them?"

"Yes."

"And based on evidence you've uncovered, you think it's possible either Mr. Bianchi is directly responsible for the deaths of all four women or someone related him, such as a scorned lover, is the killer?"

"You're batting a thousand. So, what do you think? Do you think we have a viable theory? Wanda's daughter told me Bianchi has women in every city he visits every month. I would think that might cause some ruffled feathers."

Salinger paused. I could hear him breathing, so I knew we hadn't lost our connection. Eventually, he spoke. "Perhaps. Although if he's as open about his relationships as you make it sound, I'm sure the women knew what they were getting into when they signed on with him in the first place. Still, I want to explore this line of reasoning further. I'll need a copy of the file you stumbled on to. I can pick it up if you like."

"I need to go see a woman about a dog. I have a copy of the file with me. I'll make another for you and drop it off on my way."

"Exactly how many copies of this file are floating around out there?"

"Including the one I plan to make for you?"

"Yes, including mine."

I cringed. "Five."

"Five!" Salinger shot back.

"I have one, Hazel has one, Zak has one, Ethan has one, and now you'll have one."

Salinger let out a long sigh. "Promise me you won't make a copy for anyone else."

"I promise. I'll be by your office in twenty minutes."

Salinger was waiting in the reception area when Charlie and I arrived. He escorted us back to his office after instructing his receptionist not to disturb us unless it was an emergency. I sat down across from him at his desk and handed him the file. I took a minute to explain what we'd learned about each victim while he thumbed through it.

"Our current theory," I began, "is that all four deaths—Willa's, Wanda's, Tamara's, and Gwen's—come back to Anthony Bianchi. We've learned he has businesses in Ashton Falls, where Willa died, Boston, where Wanda died, San Francisco, where Tamara died, and Portland, where Gwen died. We haven't found a direct link between Bianchi and Gwen yet, but we know Wanda died after running into the wall of a building Bianchi owned, Willa was dumped at the doorstep of one of his restaurants, and the tainted soup eaten by Tamara was purchased from another. There are too many links to make them random."

Salinger tossed the file he had been looking at on top of his desk. "I agree. I'll do some digging to see what I can come up with. I should be able to pull the original police reports for the first three victims. Maybe something will pop out as being relevant."

"Zak is decorating today, so he isn't working on the file right now, and I have a ton of errands to do, so I doubt I'll get to it either. You might check with Ethan. He seemed pretty gung ho to get going on it when I spoke to him last night."

"I'll call him to see if he has anything. This is good work, but remember your promise to Zak: no sleuthing unless someone is with you."

"I remember. I'm not sleuthing. In fact, other than some errands for the Zoo, the only thing on my schedule today is lunch with Ellie and a Halloween dance."

******

I decided to leave Charlie in the car when I arrived at the home of Matilda's neighbor. I wasn't sure what to expect, and Matilda had never filed a formal complaint, but there was no way I was going to sit around and do nothing if a dog's life was at risk. I'd brought some literature on training dogs not to bark using reinforcement for desired behavior, but the success of these types of interventions totally depended on the dog owner. If they were unwilling or unable to take the time needed to train the dog not to bark, a bark collar or removal of the pet from the home were really the only answers. Unfortunately, removal from the home required a lot of steps, beginning with a written complaint by a neighbor that, unfortunately, I didn't have.

I could hear the dog barking at the back of the house as I stepped onto the porch. The sound grew nearer after I rang the bell. From the front of the house, the sound didn't seem too bad, but I could see where the left side of the dog owner's home and the right side of Matilda's were very close in the back of the structures. If Matilda's bedroom was in the spot with the least clearance between the houses, and she slept with her window open, I could imagine the dog waking her in the middle of the night.

"Can I help you?" A woman with curlers in her hair answered the door.

"My name is Zoe. I'm here on behalf of animal control. We've had a complaint about your dog barking late at night."

"That witch from next door sic you on me? I told her what was gonna happen if she opened her flap to the cops."

"Mrs. …" I paused, hoping the woman would fill in the blank.

She didn't.

"I'm here to try to work out a solution that will satisfy you both. I know you love your dog, but there are laws regarding prolonged barking. I'm sure you understand how a dog with a propensity to bark at all hours could be annoying to those who live nearby."

"My dog has the right to do in her own home what she sees fit. If the witch next door doesn't like it she can move."

The woman started to close the door. I stuck my foot in the jamb and was rewarded with a smashed toe. "Look," I began in a much firmer tone, "I don't know what your issue with your neighbor is, but I'm here to tell you that I have the legal right to remove your dog from your home if you're unable or unwilling to get the barking under control." I forced the pamphlets I'd brought into the woman's hands. "You should consider this visit a warning. I'll be monitoring the situation. If you'd like help coming up with a management plan please call the number on the pamphlet and a professional dog trainer will call to make an appointment to speak with you."

The woman threw the pamphlets back in my face, gave me a shove so I would clear the doorway, and then slammed the door. There wasn't a lot I could do without an official complaint from an affected neighbor. If Matilda wouldn't file one I'd have Jeremy visit other neighbors in the area. There was no way I was going to risk Matilda following through with her threat to poison the dog without doing everything in my power to find another way.

******

I dropped Charlie back at the Zoo and then headed into town to meet Ellie, who was waiting for me at Rosie's when I arrived. She'd suggested a different restaurant, but you know me; I'm always looking for an opportunity to pick up random pieces of information when there's a mystery to solve. The restaurant wasn't too crowded, so Ellie had settled into a booth near the window.

"Where's Eli?" I asked.

"At your parents'. I was going to bring him, but your mom dropped by to give me some toys Harper had outgrown and she thought Eli might enjoy. When I told her I was meeting you for lunch she volunteered to take him to her house to play for an hour. You're lucky to have her so close. She's going to be a huge help to you once Catherine's born."

I took a sip of my water. "Mom is great, but I do sometimes wonder if I shouldn't agree to a full-time nanny, as Zak suggested."

"Zak wants you to hire a nanny?"

"I don't think he cares whether we have one or not, but he's really busy and he knows I don't want to give up my work at the Zoo, at least not any more than I already have. I've considered bringing Catherine to the Zoo with me, but there are times I need to go out on a call and I don't want to drag her all over town. Given our lifestyle, a nanny makes sense, but then I think about someone else raising my baby and realize I don't want that either. I'm really conflicted."

"It's hard to find a good balance after you have a baby," Ellie admitted. "I love being home with Eli, but there are times I find myself dreaming of doing something just for me."

"Like what?" I asked.

Ellie shrugged. "I don't know for sure. I've thought about opening another restaurant, but that really would be a demanding undertaking, and I don't necessarily want to work for someone else who'll require me to punch a clock. I like having flexibility in my schedule to spend time with Eli, but I'd like to have a part-time project I can sink my teeth in to. Financially, Levi and I are doing okay on his salary, so I'm not really in a hurry to decide, but it's been on my mind. I guess I'll just think about it a bit and see if any opportunities arise."

"I'm glad we're doing this baby thing together," I commented. "At least we have each other to talk to. It helps."

Ellie squeezed my hand. "Yeah, it really does."

The waitress came to take our order, so our conversation paused. I ordered a Cobb salad, while Ellie tried to decide between a sandwich and the special of the day. I watched the manager out of the corner of my eye as she chatted with a woman who looked familiar but I couldn't place. I never had gotten around to speaking to Ginger about Willa's death, but at this point I wasn't even sure what I wanted to ask. I'd been told she didn't get along with

Willa, but a lot of people didn't get along with Willa. Given the file and the other deaths, it seemed there was something larger going on than a single death in Ashton Falls, so I had no reason to suspect Ginger of any wrongdoing.

"See the woman Ginger's speaking to?" I whispered to Ellie after the waitress left.

Ellie turned her head.

"Doesn't she look familiar to you?" I asked.

Ellie shook her head. "No. I don't think I've ever seen her before. Why?"

I narrowed my gaze and tried to focus on where I'd met her, but nothing was coming to me. "I don't know. She just seems familiar."

"Given the fact that it's barely fall and she's all bundled up in that huge turtleneck, I'm going to guess she's from out of this area. Most likely somewhere with a warmer climate."

I watched as the man I now recognized as Anthony Bianchi walked into the restaurant, kissed the woman on the cheek, and sat down across from her. A visitor in town who just happened to know the man I suspected was linked to four deaths was someone I very much wanted to get to know more about.

Chapter 14

After meeting Hillary and her mother to take care of the adoption paperwork I headed home. My mom would be by in a couple of hours to help Alex get ready and I wanted a chance to speak with Zak about the case before we were otherwise occupied for the remainder of the day.

"The place looks totally awesome," I complimented as soon as I arrived.

"Thanks." Zak grinned. "I'm pretty happy with the way things turned out. How was your lunch?"

"It was nice. Ellie and I talked about babies, nannies, and life after delivery."

"Are you considering the nanny idea?"

I paused. "I'm not sure. I figure we don't need to make a decision right away, and after speaking to Ellie I think I'm pretty sure I want to wait and see how I feel about things after Catherine's born."

Zak began picking up his tools and returning them to his toolbox. "I guess that makes sense. We both have flexible jobs, so we may be able to make it work without regular help, but if we decide we need it the option is always open to us."

"That's basically the conclusion I came to as well."

"Did you go by to see Salinger?" Zak asked, changing the subject.

"Yes. I shared the file with him, although I didn't tell him where I'd gotten it. He seemed to think we could be on to something, but he wasn't totally convinced the deaths of the three women had anything to do with hers. Still, he's looking in to them. He may even call to speak to you about them at some point."

Zak picked up his toolbox and headed toward the toolshed. I followed behind. "If the four deaths in San Francisco, Boston, Portland, and Ashton Falls are related, someone—perhaps Anthony Bianchi—must have been in all four places on the corresponding dates. I can hack into his credit card statements to take a peek. If he wasn't there we'll know it wasn't him."

"We know he was in Ashton Falls when Willa died, so we just need to prove the other three locations." I paused and frowned. "The thing that's bugging me about the theory that he's the killer is why? Even if he *was* sleeping with all these women why kill them? And then there's the skin under Willa's fingernails. Salinger said it's from a Caucasian female. If Bianchi killed the women, who fought with Willa? It seems to me that if the deaths are related the killer won't be Bianchi but someone, perhaps a scorned lover, out to make a statement by eliminating the man's women one at a time."

Zak replaced the small toolbox on the shelf, then locked the shed. "You make a good point, although we only know for certain that Bianchi was involved in a sexual relationship with Wanda. Maybe our first step should be to explore the link between him and the women who died in San Francisco and Portland."

"I agree." I looked toward the horizon. "My mom will be here soon and then we have the dance, but maybe we can work on this later."

Zak took my hand and started back toward the house. "I'll check out a few things while you get Alex ready. Maybe we can figure this out by the time the others get here tonight."

******

"If you want your hair curled you'll need to sit still," Mom said to Alex later that afternoon.

"Sorry. I'm not used to having someone else do my hair. Do you think all those little ringlets are the best way to go?"

"Once we get the ringlets into your hair we'll finger comb it and they'll relax, creating gentle waves. Trust me," Mom answered. "You're going to look beautiful."

Alex looked nervous and I agreed that tight curls didn't fit her personality, but my mom seemed to know what she was doing and we could always wet it and brush it out if it didn't turn out as she hoped.

"Ellie and I stopped by the fabric store after lunch," I said to distract Alex, who looked like she was about to jump off the stool Mom had her sitting on. "We found some adorable fabric for the nursery. Ellie's going to make a quilt for the crib and a pad cover for the changing table."

"That's wonderful," Mom said as she put the final curls in Alex's hair. "Did you decide on a shade of paint?"

"Jeremy is working on a diagram of the mural he's going to paint. Once he works out all the colors he's going to suggest a shade for the other walls. He's promised no pink, so I trust him to come up with something that will work."

"I love the baby animal idea," Alex said, visibly relaxing as she joined in the conversation. "I have a couple picked out online that I'm going to buy for Catherine for Christmas."

"Catherine isn't due until after Christmas," I pointed out.

"She exists, so she needs a gift," Alex argued. "Besides, sometimes babies come early. It's best to be prepared."

Suddenly, I started to panic. I'd come to grips with the idea of giving birth after the first of the year, but before Christmas? I'd never be ready.

"There," Mom said as she stood back and looked at Alex.

"Wow," I said as I looked at the beautiful and suddenly very mature-looking young woman sitting in front of me.

"Does it look okay?" Alex asked.

Mom turned her stool so she was facing the mirror.

"I look so different," Alex said.

She wasn't wrong.

"Do you like it?" Mom asked.

Alex grinned. "I do. I didn't think I would, but I really do." She turned and hugged my mom.

"Great," Mom said. "Now, let's put on the dress."

******

The dance was well attended and a lot of fun. Alex not only looked like a princess but she seemed to have a good time once she relaxed. I could see Zak was keeping an eagle eye on Alex and Mark the entire evening, but it seemed obvious to me the two classmates were just friends and Papa Zak had nothing to worry about. Scooter was staying overnight with Tucker and Alex had decided to spend the night with Eve and Pepper, two of the students living with Phyllis, so Zak and I returned home to a childless mansion. It was too bad Hazel and the rest of the sleuthing gang were on their way over. It had been a long time since Zak and I had had the house to ourselves.

"Thank you all for coming by so late in the evening," I said when everyone arrived. "I think we should make this brief; we all have busy days tomorrow. Who wants to start?"

"I will," Ethan volunteered as Zak, Hazel, Grandpa, Phyllis, and I looked on. "I spent a good amount of time today researching each of the three victims who were mentioned in the file. While I don't feel I can conclusively say the three deaths are related to one another, Anthony Bianchi, and Willa, I do think there's a justification for considering it a real possibility." Ethan took a breath, then continued. "According to what Wanda's daughter told Zoe, Willa's sister was living with Bianchi when he died. We also know Bianchi lived in Boston, which, I assume, is where he spent most of his time, although he did travel extensively. Based on what Zoe was told, Wanda knew of Bianchi's other women and either didn't mind or, at the very least, chose to ignore them."

Ethan picked up his copy of the file and considered the contents. "Wanda was killed three weeks ago when the car she was driving swerved and hit a wall. According to the witnesses quoted in Willa's file, she swerved to avoid hitting a dog, which would seem to demonstrate the incident really was nothing more than a terrible accident. I found an additional newspaper article from a rival source. According to it, Wanda did swerve to avoid hitting a dog, but she was able to correct and continue on. and it was actually an oncoming car that crossed over from the other lane that caused her to swerve once again and hit the wall."

"If it was an oncoming car that caused the accident it could have been intentional," I said when Ethan paused.

It was at this point that Zak jumped in. "I pulled the original police report. It confirms what Ethan said. Wanda was driving along at a fair rate of speed when a dog ran out in front of her. She swerved to avoid hitting the dog but seemed to have corrected until a car in the oncoming lane swerved into her lane and she ended up hitting the wall of a building we already know was owned by Anthony Bianchi."

"What about the others?" Hazel asked.

Ethan glanced at me and I nodded.

"The first victim, Tamara Stewart, died because she came into contact with peanut oil that had been added to her soup, which came from a restaurant she frequently dined at and had recently worked for. The restaurant was owned by Bianchi, and from the evidence I could gather, she'd only recently quit her job when Bianchi's personal assistant retired and he offered it to her."

"So she gets what sounds like a huge promotion and then someone kills her shortly after," I summarized.

"It would seem. According to statements given by friends, Tamara never went anywhere without her EpiPen. She had one in her purse and she kept another in her car. According to those friends, there was no reason for her to not have had access to the epinephrine when she needed it."

"So someone at the restaurant must have tampered with the soup," I concluded.

"And because the EpiPens had been removed from Tamara's purse and car, the killer must have known she was going to come by to order the soup," Hazel added.

"Her killer, assuming there is one and Tamara's death wasn't the result of a series of unfortunate incidents, had to have been someone who knew her fairly well," Grandpa jumped in. "They would have needed not only to have access to her purse and car but to know her plans for the evening."

"If she used to work at the restaurant and continued to work for Bianchi, she would have known the entire staff," Phyllis pointed out. "It could have been any of them."

I shook my head. "No, I don't think so. If we're operating under the assumption that all the deaths are related, it's more likely the killer would be someone from Tamara's new job. What about Gwen Farmer? Did you find a link between her and Bianchi?"

"I did," Ethan confirmed. "Gwen died five weeks ago in a house fire. Her remains were found in her bed. The cause of the fire was reported as faulty wiring in the newspaper."

"Actually," Zak interrupted, "I pulled the police report for that incident as well. While it was never leaked to the press, the cause of death was blunt force trauma and the official cause of the fire was arson. The investigation is still ongoing and the police are keeping the details from the public."

"Blunt force trauma?" I asked. "Does that mean she was dead before the fire even started?"

"Due to a lack of smoke in her lungs, that's exactly what it means. The current theory is that she died as the result of a head injury and the fire was created to serve as a smoke screen."

I returned my attention to Ethan. "And her connection to Bianchi?"

"He'd been discussing with her the job opening created when Tamara died," Ethan informed us.

"Bingo," Grandpa said. "We have a link to Bianchi for all the women."

"It doesn't make sense that Bianchi was killing these women," Phyllis inserted.

"No, it doesn't," I agreed. "What does make sense is that someone close to Bianchi was killing the women to send a message to him. First, the woman he hired as his personal assistant was killed, then the woman he was discussing filling the job with died. A couple of weeks after that, the woman he was living with was run off the road, and three weeks later a childhood friend was found wrapped in a blanket and dumped on the doorstep of one of his restaurants. Someone is going all single white female on the guy."

"But who?" Hazel asked.

"It has to be someone who was in all four locations when the deaths occurred." I glanced at Zak. "We need to get a list of his employees, his women, his friends. We have to figure out who might have motive and then we track their movements to see if they were in all the locations where the women died."

"We should fill Salinger in," Zak commented.

"Yeah. I'll text him and ask him to call me if he's still awake."

"Wouldn't you think Mr. Bianchi knows who is doing this?" Phyllis asked. "He is obviously intelligent. He must have realized the deaths were all linked to him. And he must have an idea who would have had access to all four women."

I nodded. "Good point."

"If he knows why hasn't he turned them in?" Grandpa asked.

"He must be in on it," Hazel concluded.

"If he is we're back to why," I said. "The whole thing makes no sense."

"Maybe he does know who's doing it but has a reason not to turn the person in," Zak offered. "Maybe the killer has something on him. The deaths were a way to get his attention, perhaps even to remind Bianchi that he isn't the one calling the shots."

"So we're looking at one of those do-as-I-say-or-someone-important-to-you-dies scenarios?" I asked.

"It sort of fits," Zak answered. "Maybe Bianchi knows who it is but feels helpless to stop them. He doesn't turn them in to the cops for fear of retribution."

"So how do we figure out who this person might be?" I asked.

Everyone sat in silence. I assumed everyone was as stumped as I was.

"The first three deaths were made to look like accidents," Ethan eventually said. "Willa's death was different. She was obviously murdered, and the fact that she was left at the back door of Rosie's seems an intentional move to link Bianchi to the murder. It seems as if the killer is getting bolder. More desperate. Maybe Bianchi is resisting the killer's attempt to control him. My guess is that they'll strike again. Do we know if Bianchi is still in town?"

"I saw him at Rosie's today," I answered.

"We need to find out who he's been in contact with since he's been in town," Zak stated. "If Bianchi is still in town the chances are the killer is as well."

There was a murmur of agreement within the group.

"I have one more thing," Ethan said. "I'm not sure if it's related or not."

"Okay," I said. "What'd you find?"

"I spoke to Salinger while doing my research to ask a few questions and run some theory by him. He told me that you found a photo in Willa's house of four children: Willa, Wanda, TJ—which we now know is the nickname used by Antony Bianchi—and a girl named Ginny."

"That's correct. Wanda's daughter Stephi told me that Ginny developed some sort of personality disorder when she was younger and was institutionalized. She isn't certain what became of her."

"I was curious, so I decided to do some digging," Ethan continued. "It seems Ginny was diagnosed with schizophrenia when she was in her late teens. She was treated as an outpatient for a while when she had a child, a daughter. Shortly after, it was decided she was an unfit mother, so the daughter was put into the foster care system and Ginny was institutionalized."

"Wow; that's really tragic," I said. "Do you know what became of either the mother or daughter?"

"Ginny, who lived out the remainder of her life in the institution, died a year ago. She committed suicide. The daughter, Vivian, was eventually adopted by a family named Sutcliff. The Sutcliffs seemed to be a stable yet financially lacking family. Vivian, however, managed to earn a scholarship to college and eventually was awarded an MBA."

"It sounds like she did okay despite her rough beginnings," I said.

"It seems she did. The only reason I even brought it up is because it turns out

Vivian's father is none other than Anthony Bianchi."

The room fell silent.

"He had a daughter?" I clarified even though I'd just heard it with my own ears.

"He did."

"Did he know about her?"

Ethan nodded. "Initially, he gave money to Ginny to help with Vivian's support. After Ginny was institutionalized he was offered custody, which he decided to sign away. The girl was put into foster care and eventually adopted by the Sutcliffs. I have no idea if she knows who her father is, but if she does, it seems to me she might hold a pretty big grudge against the man who abandoned her and her mother when they needed him the most."

Suddenly, it seemed, we had a new suspect to add to the list.

Chapter 15

Saturday, October 28

While I really wanted to do some digging into the information Zak and Ethan had presented the previous evening, there were a couple hundred kids waiting to play games and win prizes at the kiddie carnival. Luckily, all my volunteers showed up and it appeared several of them brought spouses and friends to help as well.

"Where's Zak?" Levi asked shortly after the gates opened and the crowd descended on us.

"He took Scooter and Tucker over to the corn maze and then he was going to stop by the food court to make sure everyone who'd agreed to provide food showed up. He has his cell if you need him."

"We could use some more volunteers for the dunking tank, but I'll look elsewhere. Did Ellie stop by to give you the updated time schedule before she headed over to the bake-off?"

"She did. I agree it makes sense to combine the cookies and pastries into a single event, given that we're short on help."

Levi looked down at his clipboard. "I'm sure someone will complain, but it seems those who complain the loudest are the ones who never volunteer to help out. If your parents come by with Eli tell them to bring him by the haunted house."

"Don't you think he's a little young for the haunted house?" I asked.

"I built a mini-event in one room with bright colors and mechanical pumpkins for the little guys. If his reaction to the Frankenstein Ellie bought is any indication I think he'll love it."

I had to smile as Levi jogged away. Pre-Eli, Levi would never in a million years have even thought to create a play area for the toddlers of Ashton Falls.

A quick circuit of the area confirmed that all the booths I was responsible for were staffed and stocked with plenty of prizes. My back was bothering me this morning, so I decided to take a break in the shade. I'd noticed a bench had been set under a tree along the back perimeter of the carnival, so it was in that direction I headed.

I sat down on the bench and called Salinger. I'd left him a detailed message regarding our meeting the previous evening, but he hadn't yet called me back.

"Donovan," he answered.

"Did you get my message?"

"I did. I was just about to call you. I did some more digging…"

"Hang on," I interrupted as I noticed someone walking in my direction. "I'll call you back."

With that, I hung up and slipped the phone into my pocket.

The woman walking in my direction was the same one I'd seen in Rosie's yesterday. Suddenly, I knew why she looked so familiar. She looked exactly like her mother.

"Excuse me," I said after leaving the bench and intercepting the woman, who was wearing another turtleneck.

"Yes?" The woman paused.

"Are you Vivian?" I asked.

The woman frowned. "Do I know you?"

I shook my head. "No. My name is Zoe. I saw a photo of your mother in Willa's house and I must say, you look exactly like your mother."

The woman's eyes narrowed and her face hardened. "I can assure you, I'm nothing like my mother. Now, if you'll excuse me, I'm meeting someone."

I felt my stomach knot in warning, but I ignored it. "I saw you with TJ. I wondered if the two of you had ever established a relationship. I'm happy to see you found each other."

She moved slightly so my back was against a large tree and she stood in front of me. "You seem to know a lot about my family. Why is that?"

I shrugged, trying to appear nonchalant. "I told you, Willa was a friend of mine. I saw the photo of your parents, along with Willa and Wanda, and was curious, so I asked about it."

"Willa didn't know TJ was my father. No one did. So, again, I ask, how did you?"

Oops. It appeared I'd overplayed my hand. Where had Ethan gotten that information if it wasn't from public records? I supposed I should have asked.

"I'm sure Willa told me," I lied. "I guess she found out somehow. It was nice meeting you, but I need to be going."

Vivian grabbed my arm. "Not so fast. I find I have a few more questions."

I tried to pull away, but Vivian was remarkably strong and pulled me toward the tree line, where those attending the Hamlet would be less likely to see us. I dug in my heels and stood my ground. There was no way I was going to take a walk with this woman in that forest. "I'm sorry, but I have to go."

Vivian moved her free hand into her pocket to reveal a small gun. "Move," she said again.

I turned and took a step forward. "Wait," I said, leaning over and pretending to dry heave. I slipped my hand into my pocket, found my phone, and hit redial. Hopefully, Salinger would pick up and hear what was going on. I could try to wrestle the gun out of the woman's hand, but I didn't want to do anything that could risk injury to Catherine.

"Are you quite finished?" Vivian asked after a moment.

I stood up and pretended to have stomach cramps. "I'm sorry. I'm pregnant. I think something's wrong. I just need a minute."

"Times up." She poked the gun in my back and shoved me forward.

"I guess wearing that huge orange turtleneck on a mild autumn day was the only way to cover the scratch marks on your neck," I blurted out. If she wasn't going to voluntarily tell me what was going on, I'd need to goad her into doing it.

She didn't respond.

"I've been looking for scratches on a face," I said. "It didn't occur to me to look at necks as well."

Come on, Salinger.

"I do understand why you might hold a grudge against your father," I added as we continued our trek into the woods. "It seems he bailed on you and your mother when you needed him most. He left the poor woman in an institution all those years. Not cool."

"Damn right I hold a grudge. But not because my mother died in that institution after he locked her away and never looked back. I hold a grudge because he left me to be adopted by people who were barely able to put food on the table. I was poor and he was rich. It wasn't right. I deserve to have what's coming to me."

I slowed my steps, hoping to give Salinger, provided he'd answered and knew what was going on, a chance to catch up. "I agree. You do deserve more than the lot in life you were served. But why kill Willa and the others?"

"He wouldn't listen," she screamed.

I cringed at the rage in the woman's voice. There was no way I was getting out of this alive if someone didn't intervene.

"I worked hard, went to college, and earned an MBA all on my own," she continued. "I wanted to prove to my father I wasn't my mother's daughter. I wasn't weak and sick like she was. I was strong and intelligent. I thought if I could find a way to earn his love he would welcome me into his life. So I busted my ass and worked harder than anyone ever has. After I got my MBA I went to his office, told him who I was, and asked for a job. You know what he told me? After all I'd done to prove my worth he told me all entry-level positions were handled by personnel and I should go fill out an application."

"Wow. That's really harsh." I found myself sympathizing with her. I stopped walking, but she was on a rant and didn't seem to notice.

"I reminded him that I wasn't some person off the street. I was his daughter and he owed me. He told me that he didn't owe me a thing, but he liked my spunk. He offered me a job in personnel and promised he'd keep me in mind if something opened up in the corporate office. I couldn't wait around for someone to quit. I had my foot in the door and knew I needed to strike while the iron was hot."

"So you went to San Francisco, where his new personal assistant was visiting the restaurant where she used to work, and you killed her."

"I had to."

The woman's logic was severely flawed, but I didn't want to make her madder than she already was, so I agreed. "I suppose it was easy to find out about the peanut allergy. It would have been in her personnel file. I have to assume that even though you created an opening for the position you wanted he didn't offer it to you."

"No, he didn't. I had an MBA and I was his daughter and he had me doing clerical work. When he went to Portland to speak to the woman he had his eye on for the assistant position, I realized the job was slipping between my fingers, so I took care of her as well, only this time I made sure he knew exactly what I'd done. I figured he'd realize I was serious about being his assistant and would give me the job I deserved. I was sure he wasn't going to risk another death by giving the job to someone else, but instead of hiring me, he decided not to fill the position. Like that would stop me. The man had to be made to see I would do anything to get what I deserved."

"So you killed his girlfriend," I said, referring to Wanda.

"One of them. He had others. I didn't think he'd even miss her. I tried to tell him the accident was all about me, but he insisted Wanda was killed after she swerved to avoid hitting a dog. Not only did he not believe I'd killed her, he began to doubt I'd killed the others. He thought I was being delusional. I had to make him see it was me who'd killed all those women. He needed to understand that if he didn't want others to end up like the first four he'd better give me what I wanted."

I noticed Salinger along with Zak walking slowly toward us from behind Vivian. She didn't seem to notice, but I needed to keep her talking. "So you delivered Willa to your father all wrapped up like a giant present."

Vivian smiled. "You realized the significance of the blanket. My so-called father totally missed it. But he did finally realize I was serious about getting my way and he finally promoted me to the position I deserve. We leave today."

I knew I just needed a few more seconds and Zak and Salinger would be in position. "I can see you're serious about getting what you want. I have to say I admire that. Good luck in your new venture."

Vivian raised the gun and pointed it at my head. "You know, I like you. I'm sorry I have to kill you, but you know I can't let you live."

"I understand."

"Zoe," Zak called from behind a tree.

Vivian turned to look behind her a split second before Salinger tackled her. I heard a shot and looked frantically at myself, but I seemed to be uninjured. I looked at Salinger, who pulled Vivian to her feet. Both appeared to be fine. I then glanced at Zak, who was walking toward me with blood covering the front of his shirt.

Chapter 16

Tuesday, October 31

It seemed the entire town had shown up for the funeral, which was held the previous afternoon. It had been a cold, drizzly day, but that hadn't stopped anyone from showing up to pay their last respects. It was times like this that it hit me how delicate and unpredictable life was.

"You okay?" Ellie asked as I stared into the distance.

"I'm fine. Just thinking about things that could have been."

Ellie wove her fingers through mine. "Yeah. It's been a tough week. The party turned out nice, though."

"I hated to cancel. I thought about it, but Zak worked so hard on it."

"Everything was perfect, and I think we could all use some fun in our lives. I need to go check on Eli. If you need to talk I'll be upstairs."

I hugged Ellie. "Okay, thanks."

I called to Charlie, who seemed intent on following me everywhere, and headed outside to check on the kids. The spooky graveyard, complete with fog machine, was a huge hit with the younger kids and the teens from Zimmerman Academy as well. The sun had set and the yard had grown dark except for the orange lights overhead. I stood off to the side with Charlie with me. The laughter from the kids enjoying Zak's effort made the heaviness in my heart a little lighter.

"I think you have a hit on your hands." Levi came over and put his arm around my waist.

"It would seem."

"I have to hand it to Zak. It's even better than the haunted house at the Hamlet this year, and that was pretty awesome, if I do say so myself."

I leaned over and kissed Levi on the cheek. "This is pretty great, but the haunted house was awesome too. You did a wonderful job, my friend."

"Have you seen Ellie?" Levi asked.

"Inside, checking on Eli."

Levi squeezed my shoulder one last time, then headed toward the house. A couple of kids from the high school tried to pull him into the graveyard, but he managed to tackle them and get by. I looked down at Charlie. "Should we go see what Harper and Morgan are up to?" My sister had dressed as the most adorable spider, while Jeremy's daughter, Morgan, was a cuddly lion cub.

"Not so fast." I felt an arm wrap around my waist from behind.

I turned and looked at Zak. "What are you doing out here? I thought the doctor told you to take it easy."

"I couldn't miss my own haunted graveyard, could I?"

"Actually, you could. If it had been me that had been shot you would have insisted on it."

"I'm not you and I'm not pregnant. Besides, I'm fine. The bullet barely left a scratch."

"Trust me, I was there. It was more than a scratch." I lightly touched the spot where I knew the bandage on Zak's chest was located. "If the bullet had been fired at closer range or if it had landed a little to the left, you could have died. For a minute

223

there, I thought you *would* die. I never want to go through that again."

"I know. I'm sorry you had to go through it the first time." Zak turned me around with his left arm because his right one was in a sling. "I hate that you were so scared, but I think the thing to remember is that I didn't die."

"You should be resting."

"I'm not tired."

"It doesn't matter whether you're tired; the doctor said you needed to take it easy. I left you sitting in your comfy chair and you promised to stay put."

"I got bored."

I let out a growl of frustration. Who knew Zak would be such a difficult patient?

He leaned closer and kissed me gently on the lips. Then he pulled back a bit and looked me in the eye. "It's a beautiful night. The kids are occupied and our guests are all having fun. Now, do you really want to fight or do you want to walk down to the beach with me?"

I was about to march the crazy man standing in front of me into the house and back into the chair where I'd left him when he began kissing my neck.

"So what do you say?" I could feel Zak's lips against me. "Just you and me under the moonlight."

"There's no moon."

"Even better," Zak said as he continued to kiss my neck.

I let out a soft groan. "I really should march you inside, but I guess a short walk on the beach would be okay."

Zak found my lips, and suddenly the heaviness in my heart faded away. I'd miss Willa and was sad she'd no longer be in my life, but I did feel good that we'd found her killer and justice would be served. Not only was Vivian in jail, awaiting a trial for four counts of first-degree murder plus one count of attempted murder but Anthony Bianchi was in jail as well for knowing what she had done and not turning her in.

"I've been thinking about the Christmas display," Zak said as we passed by the haunted graveyard he'd set up. "What we had last year was fine, but I think this year we need to go bigger and bolder."

I rested my head on Zak's shoulder as we slowly walked toward the beach. "What's bigger and bolder than enough lights to cover the town and a horse-drawn sleigh?"

"Reindeer. Live reindeer, to be exact."

A New Series from Kathi Daley Books

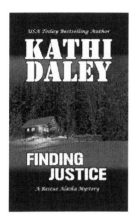

Sample Chapter for Finding Justice

There are people in the world who insist that life is what you make of it. They'll tell you that if you work hard enough and persevere long enough, everything you've ever desired will one day be yours. But as I sat in the fifth dingy office I'd visited in as many months and listened as the fifth pencil pusher in a dark suit and sensible shoes looked at me with apologetic eyes, I finally understood that not every dream was realized and not every wish granted.

"Ms. Carson, do you understand what I'm saying?"

I nodded, trying to fight back the tears I absolutely would not shed. "You're saying that you can't consider my grant application unless I've secured a facility."

The man let out a long breath that sounded like a wheeze, which I was sure was more of a sigh of relief. "Exactly. I do love your proposal to build an animal shelter in your hometown, but our grant is designed to be used for ongoing operations. I'm afraid without a physical presence we really must move on."

I leaned over to pick up my eight-year-old backpack. "Yes. I understand. Thank you so much for your time."

"Perhaps next year?" the man encouraged with a lopsided grin.

I smiled in return. Granted, it was a weak little smile that did nothing to conceal my feelings of defeat. "Thank you. I'm certain we'll be able to meet your criteria by the next application cycle."

"We begin a new cycle on June 1. If you can secure a facility by that time please feel free to reapply," the man said.

I thanked the bureaucrat and left his office. I tried to ignore the feeling of dread in the pit of my stomach and instead focused on the clickety-clack that sounded as the tile floor came into contact with the two-inch heels I'd bought for this occasion. Had I really been working on this project for more than two years? Maybe it was time to throw in the towel and accept defeat. The idea of building an animal shelter in Rescue Alaska was a noble one, but the mountain of fund-raising and paperwork that needed to be scaled to make this particular dream come true seemed insurmountable at best.

I dug into my backpack for my cell phone, which rang just as I stepped out of the warm building into the bracing cold of the frigid Alaskan winter. I pulled the hood of my heavy parka over my dark hair before wrapping its bulk tightly around my small frame.

"So, how did it go?" My best friend, Chloe Rivers, asked the minute I answered her call.

"It went."

"What happened?" Chloe groaned.

I looked up toward the sky, allowing the snow to land on my face and mask my tears. "The grant is designated for operations, so it seems we aren't eligible until we have a facility. The problem is, we have no money to build a facility and no one will give us a loan for one unless we have capital for operations already lined up. It's an endless cycle I'm afraid we can't conquer."

"We can't give up. You know what you have to do."

"No," I said firmly. "We'll find another way." I knew I sounded harsh, but I had to make Chloe understand.

"Another way?" Chloe screeched. I listened as she took a deep breath before continuing in a softer tone. "Come on, Harmony, you know we've tried everything. There *is* no other way."

Chloe's plea faded as an image flashed into my mind. I closed my eyes and focused on the image before I spoke. I knew from previous experience that it was important to get a lock on the psychic connection before I said or did anything to break the spell. Once I felt I was ready, I opened my eyes and tuned back into Chloe's chatter. I was certain she hadn't missed a beat even though I'd missed the whole thing. "Look, I have to go," I interrupted. "Someone's in trouble. I'll call you later."

I hung up with Chloe, called a cab, and then called Dani Mathews. Dani was a helicopter pilot and one of the members of the search-and-rescue team I was a part of. She'd offered to give me a lift into

Anchorage for my meeting today and I'd taken her up on it.

"Someone's in trouble," I said as soon as Dani answered.

"I was about to call you. I just got off the phone with Jake." Jake Cartwright was my boss, brother-in-law, and the leader of the search-and-rescue team. "There are two boys, one fifteen and the other sixteen. They'd been cross-country skiing at the foot of Cougar Mountain. Jake said they have a GPS lock on a phone belonging to one of the teens, so he isn't anticipating a problem with the rescue."

The cab pulled up and I slipped inside. I instructed the driver to head to the airport, then answered Dani. "The boys dropped the phone, so Jake and the others are heading in the wrong direction"

I slipped off my shoes as the cab sped away.

"Do you know where they are?" Dani asked with a sound of panic in her voice.

"In a cave." I closed my eyes and tried to focus on the image in my head. "The cave's shallow, but they're protected from the storm." I took off my heavy parka and pulled a pair of jeans out of my backpack. I cradled the phone to my ear with my shoulder as I slipped the jeans onto my bare legs.

"Where's the cave, Harm?"

I closed my eyes once again and let the image come to me. "I'd say they're about a quarter of a mile up the mountain."

"Are they okay?" Dani asked.

I took a deep breath and focused my energy. There were times I wanted to run from the images and feelings that threatened to overwhelm and destroy me, but I knew embracing the pain and fear was my destiny as well as my burden. "They're both scared, but only one of them is hurt. Call Jake and tell him to check the cave where we found Sitka," I said, referring to our search-and-rescue dog, who Jake and I had found lost on the mountain when he was just a puppy. "And send someone for Moose." I glanced out the window. The snow was getting heavier, and it wouldn't be long before we would be forbidden from taking off. "I'm almost at the airport. Go ahead and warm up the bird. I should be there in two minutes."

I hung up the phone and placed it on the seat next to me. The driver swerved as I pulled my dress over my head and tossed it to one side. I knew the pervert was watching, but I didn't have time to care as I pulled a thermal shirt out of my backpack, over my head, and across my bare chest.

"What's the ETA to the airport?" I demanded from the backseat.

"Less than a minute."

"Go on around to the entrance for private planes. I have the code to get in the gate. My friend is waiting with a helicopter."

As the cab neared the entrance, I pulled on heavy wool socks and tennis shoes. I wished I had my snow boots with me, but the tennis shoes would have to do because the boots were too heavy to carry around all day.

As soon as the cab stopped, I grabbed my phone, tossed some cash onto the front seat, and hopped out, leaving my dress and new heels behind.

"You've forgotten your dress, miss."

"Keep it," I said as I flung my backpack over my shoulder and took off at a full run for the helicopter. As soon as I got in, Dani took off. "Did you get hold of Jake?" I asked as I strapped myself in.

"I spoke to Sarge. He's manning the radio. He promised to keep trying to get through to Jake. The storm is intensifying at a steady rate. We need to find them."

"Moose?"

"Sarge sent someone for him."

I looked out the window as we flew toward rescue. A feeling of dread settled in the pit of my stomach. The storm was getting stronger and I knew that when a storm blew in without much notice it caught everyone off guard, and the likelihood of a successful rescue decreased dramatically.

The team I belonged to was one of the best anywhere, our survival record unmatched. Still, I'd learned at an early age that when you're battling Mother Nature, even the best teams occasionally came out on the losing end. I picked up the team radio Dani had tucked into the console of her helicopter, pressed the handle, and hoped it would connect me to someone at the command post.

"Go for Sarge," answered the retired army officer who now worked for Neverland, the bar Jake owned.

"Sarge, it's Harmony. Dani and I are on our way, but we won't get there in time to make a difference. I need you to get a message to Jake."

"The reception is sketchy, but don't you worry your pretty head; Sarge will find a way."

"The boys are beginning to panic. I can feel their absolute horror as the storm strengthens. The one who isn't injured is seriously thinking of leaving his friend and going for help. If he does neither of them will make it. Jake needs to get there and he needs to get there fast."

"Don't worry. I'll find a way to let Jake know. Can you communicate with the boys?"

I paused and closed my eyes. I tried to connect but wasn't getting through. "I'm trying, but so far I just have a one-way line. Is Jordan there?" Jordan Fairchild was not only a member of the team but she was also a doctor who worked for the local hospital.

"She was on duty at the hospital, but she's on her way."

"Tell her she'll need to treat hypothermia." I paused and closed my eyes once again. My instinct was to block the pain and horror I knew I needed to channel. "And anemia. The break to the femur of the injured teen is severe. He's been bleeding for a while." I used the back of my hand to wipe away the steady stream of tears that were streaking down my face. God, it hurt. The pain. The fear. "I'm honestly not sure he'll make it. I can feel his strength fading, but we have to try."

"Okay, Harm, I'll tell her."

"Is Moose there?"

"He will be by the time you get here."

I put down the radio and tried to slow my pounding heart. I wasn't sure why I'd been cursed with the ability to connect psychically with those who were injured or dying. It isn't that I could feel the pain of everyone who was suffering; it seemed only to be those we were meant to help who found their way into my radar. I wasn't entirely sure where the ability came from, but I knew when I'd acquired it.

I grew up in a warm and caring family, with two parents and a sister who loved me. When I was thirteen my parents died in an auto accident a week before Christmas. My sister Val, who had just turned nineteen, had dropped out of college, returned to Rescue Alaska, and taken over as my legal guardian. I remember feeling scared and so very alone. I retreated into my mind, cutting ties to most people except for Val, who became my only anchor to the world. When I was fifteen Val married local bar owner Jake Cartwright. Jake loved Val and treated me like a sister, and after a period of adjustment, we became a family and I began to emerge from my shell. When I was seventeen Val went out on a rescue. She got lost in a storm, and although the team had tried to find her, they'd come up with nothing but dead ends. I remember sitting at the command post praying harder than I ever had before. I wanted so much to have the chance to tell Val how much I loved her. She'd sacrificed so much for me and I wasn't sure she knew how much it meant to me.

Things hadn't looked good, even though the entire team had searched around the clock. I could hear them whispering that the odds of finding her alive were decreasing with each hour. I remember wanting to give my life for hers, and suddenly, there she was, in my head. I could feel her pain, but I also knew the prayer in her heart. I knew she was dying, but I could feel her love for me and I could feel her fighting to live. I could also feel the life draining from her body with each minute that passed.

I tried to tell the others that I knew where she was, but they thought they were only the ramblings of an emotionally distraught teenager dealing with the fallout of shock and despair. When the team eventually found Val's body exactly where and how I'd told them they would, they began to believe that I really had made a connection with the only family I'd had left in the world.

Of course, the experience of knowing your sister was dying, of feeling her physical and emotional pain as well has her fear as she passed into the next life, was more than a seventeen-year-old could really process. I'm afraid I went just a bit off the deep end. Jake, who had taken over as my guardian, had tried to help me, as did everyone else in my life at the time, but there was no comfort in the world that would undo the horror I'd experienced.

And then I met Moose. Moose is a large Maine Coon who wandered into the bar Jake owned and I worked and lived in at the time. The minute I picked up the cantankerous cat and held him to my heart, the trauma I'd been experiencing somehow melted away. I won't go so far as to say that Moose has magical powers—at least not any more than I do—but channeling people in life-and-death situations is more draining than I can tolerate, and the only one who can keep me grounded is a fuzzy Coon with a cranky disposition.

"Are you okay?" Dani asked as she glanced at me out of the corner of her eye. Her concern for my mental health was evident on her face.

"I'm okay. I'm trying to connect with the boys, but they're too terrified to let me in. It's so hard to feel their pain when you can't offer comfort."

"Can't you shut if off? I can't imagine allowing myself to actually feel and experience what those boys are."

"If I block it I'll lose them. I have to hang on. Maybe I can get through to one of them. They don't have long."

"Do you really think you have the ability to do that? To establish a two-way communication?"

I put my hand over my heart. It felt like it was breaking. "I think so. I hope so. The elderly man who was buried in the avalanche last spring told me that he knew he was in his final moments and all he could feel was terror. Then I connected and he felt at peace. It was that peace that allowed him to slow his breathing. Jordan said the only reason he was still alive when we found him was because he'd managed to conserve his oxygen."

"That's amazing."

I shrugged. I supposed I did feel good about that rescue, but I'd been involved in rescues, such as Val's, in which the victim I connected with didn't make it. I don't know why it's my lot to experience death over and over again, but it seems to be my calling, so I try to embrace it so I'm available for the victims I can save like that old man.

"The injured one is almost gone," I whispered. "They need to get to him now."

I knew tears were streaming down my fact as I gripped the seat next to me. The pain was excruciating, but needed to hang on.

Dani reached over and grabbed my hand. "We're almost there. I'm preparing to land. Sarge is waiting with Moose."

She guided the helicopter to the ground despite the storm raging around us. As soon as she landed, I opened the door, hopped out, and ran to the car, where Sarge was waiting with Moose. I pulled him into my arms and wept into his thick fur. Several minutes later I felt a sense of calm wash over me. I couldn't know for certain, but I felt as if the boy I was channeling had experienced that same calm. I looked at Sarge. "He's gone."

"I'm so sorry, Harm."

"The other one is still alive. He's on the verge of panicking and running out into the storm. Jake and the others have to get to him."

Sarge helped me into the car and we headed toward Neverland, where I knew the fate of the second boy would be revealed before the night came to an end.

Recipes

Salisbury Steak with Mushroom Gravy—
submitted by Sharon Guagliardo
Mexican Pork—submitted by Nancy Farris
Cheese Potato Chowder—submitted by
Pam Curran
Chuck Wagon Casserole—submitted by
Patty Liu

Salisbury Steak with Mushroom Gravy

Submitted by Sharon Guagliardo

1 lb. lean ground beef
10 oz. can condensed cream of mushroom soup, divided
½ cup Italian bread crumbs
1 egg, lightly beaten
½ cup frozen chopped onions
1 tsp. steak seasoning (recommended: Montreal)
1 tbs. canola oil
2 tbs. butter, divided
¼ cup cognac
8 oz. pkg. sliced fresh mushrooms
2 cups low-sodium beef broth
1 1.2-oz. packet brown gravy mix
Cooked rice, for serving

In a large bowl, combine beef, ¼ can mushroom soup, bread crumbs, egg, onions, and steak seasoning. Mix thoroughly and shape into 4 oval patties.

Heat oil and 1 tbs. butter in large skillet over medium-high heat. Brown patties on both sides and transfer to a plate.

Add remaining butter and cognac (remove pan from heat when adding cognac). Sauté mushrooms for 7 to 8 minutes. Add beef stock and whisk in gravy mix until smooth. Stir in remaining mushroom soup.

Return patties to skillet and spoon gravy over top. Cover pan and simmer for 20 to 25 minutes.
Serve over hot cooked rice.

Prep Time: 15 minutes
Cook Time: 30 minutes
Makes 4 servings

Mexican Pork

Submitted by Nancy Farris

A favorite for cold evenings!

2 tbs. olive oil
3 tbs. cornmeal
1 tbs. ancho chili powder
1 lb. pork tenderloin, trimmed and cut in ¾" pieces
2 cups coarsely chopped fresh tomatillos
1 14-oz, can chicken broth
1 4.5-oz. can chopped green chilies
1 clove garlic, chopped
1 jalapeno pepper, seeded and chopped
½ cup finely sliced green onions
¼ cup chopped fresh cilantro
3 tbs. tequila
1 lime, juiced
Salt and pepper to taste

Heat oil in nonstick skillet on medium-high heat.

Combine cornmeal and ancho powder in plastic bag. Add pork and shake until coated. Remove pork from bag, reserving the remaining cornmeal mixture, and add to skillet. Sauté until browned, about 5 minutes. Stir in the remaining cornmeal mixture and stir for another minute, stirring constantly. Stir in tomatillos, broth, green chilies, garlic, and jalapeño. Bring to a simmer and cook for about 10 minutes on medium low until the tomatillos are tender. Stir in the remaining ingredients and simmer 1–2 minutes.

I serve in bowls with refried black beans and warm flour tortillas on the side. A good margarita never hurts either!

Serves 4

Cheese Potato Chowder

Submitted by Pam Curran

4 med. potatoes, slices or diced
1 cup celery, sliced
1 cup carrots, sliced
½ cup onion, diced
2 tsp. salt
¼ tsp. pepper
4 cups water
½ cup margarine
½ cup flour
1 qt. milk
1 lb. cheddar cheese, grated
2 cups cubed ham

Boil potatoes, celery, carrots, onions, salt and pepper in water for 10 minutes, covered.

Melt margarine in pan and blend in flour, and add milk. Cook until thick and add cheese. Stir until melted.

Add to vegetables and add ham.

Serve hot and garnish with a little paprika and parsley, if desired.

Chuck Wagon Casserole

Submitted by Patty Liu

1 lb. lean ground beef
½ large onion, chopped
1 green bell pepper, med.-size, chopped
1 tsp. garlic salt
1 tbs. chili powder
1 can diced tomatoes, undrained
1 can kidney beans, drained
1 large can whole-kernel corn, drained
Pinch of ground cumin
1 tbs. Worcestershire sauce
Hot red pepper sauce to taste
Salt and pepper to taste
1 cup shredded cheddar cheese

Preheat oven to 350 degrees.
Spray a 2-qt. casserole dish with Pam
Original.

In a large skillet, brown meat until lightly
browned. Add onion, bell pepper, garlic
salt, and chili powder; stir till vegetables
are softened.

Scrape mixture into casserole dish; add tomatoes, beans, com, cumin, and Worcestershire sauce.

Season with hot sauce, salt and pepper, stir well, and bake uncovered 30 minutes.

Sprinkle cheese over top and continue to bake until top is golden brown, about 20 minutes.

Serves 6 to 8

Books by Kathi Daley

Come for the murder, stay for the romance.

Zoe Donovan Cozy Mystery:
Halloween Hijinks
The Trouble With Turkeys
Christmas Crazy
Cupid's Curse
Big Bunny Bump-off
Beach Blanket Barbie
Maui Madness
Derby Divas
Haunted Hamlet
Turkeys, Tuxes, and Tabbies
Christmas Cozy
Alaskan Alliance
Matrimony Meltdown
Soul Surrender
Heavenly Honeymoon
Hopscotch Homicide
Ghostly Graveyard
Santa Sleuth
Shamrock Shenanigans
Kitten Kaboodle
Costume Catastrophe
Candy Cane Caper
Holiday Hangover
Easter Escapade
Camp Carter
Trick or Treason
Reindeer Roundup – *December 2017*

Zimmerman Academy The New Normal
Ashton Falls Cozy Cookbook

Tj Jensen Paradise Lake Mysteries by Henery Press

Pumpkins in Paradise
Snowmen in Paradise
Bikinis in Paradise
Christmas in Paradise
Puppies in Paradise
Halloween in Paradise
Treasure in Paradise
Fireworks in Paradise – *October 2017*

Whales and Tails Cozy Mystery:

Romeow and Juliet
The Mad Catter
Grimm's Furry Tail
Much Ado About Felines
Legend of Tabby Hollow
Cat of Christmas Past
A Tale of Two Tabbies
The Great Catsby
Count Catula
The Cat of Christmas Present
A Winter's Tail
The Taming of the Tabby
Frankencat
The Cat of Christmas Future – *November 2017*

Seacliff High Mystery:

The Secret
The Curse
The Relic
The Conspiracy
The Grudge
The Shadow
The Haunting

Sand and Sea Hawaiian Mystery:

Murder at Dolphin Bay
Murder at Sunrise Beach
Murder at the Witching Hour
Murder at Christmas
Murder at Turtle Cove
Murder at Water's Edge
Murder at Midnight – *October 2017*

Writers' Retreat Southern Seashore Mystery:

First Case
Second Look
Third Strike
Fourth Victim – *October 2017*

A Tess and Tilly Cozy Mystery

The Christmas Letter – *December 2017*

Road to Christmas Romance:

Road to Christmas Past

Rescue Alaska Paranormal Mystery

Finding Justice – *November 2017*

USA Today best-selling author Kathi Daley lives in beautiful Lake Tahoe with her husband Ken. When she isn't writing, she likes to spend time hiking the miles of desolate trails surrounding her home. She has authored more than seventy-five books in eight series including: Zoe Donovan Cozy Mysteries, Whales and Tails Island Mysteries, Sand and Sea Hawaiian Mysteries, Tj Jensen Paradise Lake Series, Writers' Retreat Southern Seashore Mysteries, Rescue Alaska Paranormal Mysteries, and Seacliff High Teen Mysteries. Find out more about her books at www.kathidaley.com

Giveaway:

I do a giveaway for books, swag, and gift cards every week in my newsletter, *The Daley Weekly* **http://eepurl.com/NRPDf**

Other links to check out:
Kathi Daley Blog – publishes each Friday
http://kathidaleyblog.com
Webpage – **www.kathidaley.com**
Facebook at Kathi Daley Books –
www.facebook.com/kathidaleybooks
Kathi Daley Teen –
www.facebook.com/kathidaleyteen

Kathi Daley Books Group Page –
https://www.facebook.com/groups/5695788231468 50/
.E-mail – **kathidaley@kathidaley.com**
Goodreads –
https://www.goodreads.com/author/show/7278377. Kathi_Daley
Twitter at Kathi Daley@kathidaley –
https://twitter.com/kathidaley
Amazon Author Page –
https://www.amazon.com/author/kathidaley
BookBub –
https://www.bookbub.com/authors/kathi-daley
Pinterest – **http://www.pinterest.com/kathidaley/**

OCT 3 0 2017

South Lake Tahoe

76882795R00142

Made in the USA
Columbia, SC
18 September 2017